The Captain's Inkwell Anthology #2

_____

Edited by Brian Bourner

Captain's Inkwell 2024

Copyright © 2023 The Authors

All rights reserved. This book or any portion thereof may not be reproduced or used in any manner whatsoever without the express written permission of the publisher except for the use of brief quotations in a book review or scholarly journal.

First Printing: 2024

Imprint: Lulu.com

ISBN 9781446687611

Captain's Inkwell
c/o Newington Library,
17 Fountainhall Road
Edinburgh, Scotland EH9 2LN

Cover Image:
View of North Edinburgh and River Forth from Calton Hill
Last Page Image:
Arthur's Seat in Winter

For all those writers who have at any time been involved with the Captain's Inkwell writers group over the past fifteen years, and for new writers everywhere, who need encouragement and support, and without whom the world would be a duller and less intelligible place.

As lang as Forth weets Lothian's shore,
As lang's on Fife her billows roar,
Sae lang shall ilk whase country's dear,
To thy remembrance gie a tear.
By thee Auld Reikie thrave and grew
Delightfu' to her childer's view:
-   Robert Fergusson

"The simple fact that millions of books exist shows conclusively that none contains the truth"- Ludwig Wittgenstein

"You only live once, but if you do it right, once is enough"
– Mae West

Editor's Introduction

This is the second general anthology of work produced by The Captain's Inkwell, an Edinburgh based writers' group. The group's first anthology appeared in 2020 (ISBN 9781716947193).

The Captain's Inkwell has functioned for many years under the auspices of the Library Services of the City of Edinburgh Council, for which we are very grateful. We were originally established by one of their librarians, Jane Blewitt, in 2013 and initially based at Gracemount Library / South-East Neighbourhood Centre on the Captain's Road in Gracemount. Nowadays we meet fortnightly in Newington Library with the support of its librarian Lindsay Simpson.

The group welcomes writers and aspiring writers of any age, level of experience, or preferred writing genre. As you will see from this book's contents that means anything from fact to fiction, from fantasy to memoir. Formats vary from flash fiction to poetry and short stories to drama scripts. While the group eschews any explicitly educational role writers often find their writing benefits from the mutually supportive comments and criticism the group provides.

While it is impossible to offer pieces of writing by all present and past members of the group, - so many having at one time or another contributed to the vibrancy and wellbeing of the group, - this current selection of fifty-three short items from seventeen different writers provides a reasonable representation of the material written over recent years and read at group meetings

Several of the items in this volume have been previously published, appearing in books or literary magazines, in print and online.

Captain's Inkwell.
WRITERS' GROUP
EVERY SECOND Friday 2.30pm
IN NEWINGTON LIBRARY
Info
Newington.library@edinburgh.gov.uk
0131 529 5536
Free To Join In
Spill some ink on anything you choose.
Read your writing to the group.
Comment on pieces written by others.
Or just listen

Contents

1. Strike! *Helen Parker* — 1
2. If Only Thelma and Louise Had Had Those Boots *Annie Foy* — 3
3. Atif *Helen Parker* — 6
4. Prescient Danger *Brian Bourner* — 9
5. The Mug *John Tucker* — 12
6. A Quick trip to Tesco *Gracie Rose* — 14
7. Do Not Disturb *Stéphanie Voytier* — 17
8. A Pea-Souper *Helen Parker* — 22
9. The Garden Path *Brian Bourner* — 25
10. Dangerous Magic *Georgina Tibai* — 27
11. A Flight of Fancy *Brian Bourner* — 32
12. A Childhood *Ian Elliot* — 37
13. The Countryman *Robin King* — 39
14. Intuition Can Only Take You So Far *Gracie Rose* — 41
15. The Funeral *Robin King* — 43
16. Memories of My Grandparents *Valentina Romanazzi* — 46
17. The Ghosts are Alive and Well *Jamie Hafner* — 49
18. Cookery Lesson *Brian Bourner* — 51
19. Falling *Sheila McDougall* — 52
20. An Able Raconteur *Gracie Rose* — 53
21. After Bagpipe Music *Brian Bourner* — 54
22. No Way to Die *Sheila McDougall* — 55
23. Plague Playhouse *Brian Bourner* — 56
24. Fighting for Words *Georgina Tibai* — 57
25. After the Party *Brian Bourner* — 58
26. Friday the Thirteenth *Helen Parker* — 68
27. The Cost of Living *Annie Foy* — 72
28. Roses Are Red Dilly Dilly *Helen Parker* — 74
29. 50 Words a Day for 7 Days *Bex Stevenson* — 76
30. Gold *Helen Parker* — 78
31. Slipping Out the Fringe *Brian Bourner* — 82

32. The Day the Colours Came Together *Sylvia Simpson* 84
33. For Richer, For Poorer *Helen Parker* 86
34. The Danger of Doppelgangers *Jamie Hafner* 88
35. The Imperfect Things *Stéphanie Voytier* 91
36. Anna Procemo *John Tucker* 93
37. Tesco in Winter *Sheila McDougall* 99
38. Another Groundhog Day in Lockdown *Brian Bourner* 100
39. School Mates *Brian Bourner* 102
40. Self Control *Sheila McDougall* 103
41. The Grate is Cold *Lucy Bucknall* 104
42. Diamonds Lost and Found *Helen Parker* 106
43. The Fog *Sylvia Simpson* 107
44. No Room *Sheila McDougall* 108
45. Winter is Coming *Sheila McDougall* 108
46. Lady Luck *or* Not Every Disability is Visible *Helen Parker* 109
47. The Rider *Brian Bourner* 111
48. A Lovely Sandwich *Maitiu Corbett* 118
49. It Wisnae Me *John Tucker* 125
50. In Days of Covid *Brian Bourner* 127
51. Treasure *Helen Parker* 128
52. Weekend Away *Janice Gardner* 130
53. Speaking of the Dead *Brian Bourner* 136

NOTES ON AUTHORS 137

STRIKE!

by Helen Parker

'Strike out! Take your courage in both hands,' Meg cajoled.

Sally didn't smile. She stood on the balcony of their flat, twenty floors up, and gazed down at the gridlocked traffic in their adopted third world city. 'At least the horn-honking is less obtrusive up here,' she sighed. 'But how do you get used to it? How do you dare to drive here? I mean, how do you even cross the road without feeling your life is on the line?'

'Ah, be brazen! Hold up an imperious hand, exude the confidence you don't feel, place your palm on the bonnet of each car as you weave your way between them. If you imagine the cars stopping for you, they will.'

Sally shuddered. 'But the pavements...'

'I know. The residents like to make sure they're impassable. They park cars on them, pile them knee-high with smelly rubbish...'

'Yes, the rats!'

'Exactly. Or they use them as an extension for shops and cafes...'

'And they restrict access to them by double-parking, bumper to bumper, especially on street corners.'

'You've got it!'

Sally was beginning to smile now, but she added, 'I'll never drive here, not in a million years.'

'Oh, driving's a piece of cake once you've understood the highway code.'

'The highway code?'

'Yep. Ignore traffic lights, zebra crossings and speed limits. Seatbelts are for wimps. Never use indicators - you'll lose that surprise factor.'

She kept a serious face, despite Sally's open-mouthed shock. 'Turn left from the right-hand lane, and vice-versa. Maintain that element of surprise by changing lanes frequently and at random. Never use headlights at night - they might warn other road users of your approach.'

Sally's tentative smile was returning.

'Aim for easy targets, for example, cyclists riding against the flow of traffic, especially on one-way streets. Look out for motorcyclists with at least 5 passengers - their balance may be affected.'

She lowered her voice and added, 'Avoid the 5% wearing helmets.'

Sally was chuckling now.

'Practise multitasking: save your most interesting cell-phone calls for when you're driving. At night, approach pedestrians on dark side streets slowly and quietly, then honk your horn as you draw alongside them. With a bit of luck, they'll jump right in front of you.'

'And if you score by knocking down a pedestrian,' Sally added, 'never stop the car. His relatives may leap out and lynch you.'

'Bravo! You're almost a native. The locals would be proud of you.'

Meg looked out from the balcony. 'Look, it's Asr - early evening prayer. The traffic has eased a bit. Let's head out now and strike while the iron's hot.'

IF ONLY THELMA AND LOUISE HAD HAD THOSE BOOTS

by Annie Foy

She was in the yard scrubbing overalls in the tub. The washing machine stopped working two months ago and she couldn't repair it. It was as old as Methuselah's granny: no way of finding replacement parts now, no money for a new one. Her temper, like her fingernails was frayed. She was fit to be tied when the truck pulled up and the most beautiful pair of embroidered western boots, gold over shining black, slid out.

"Last time I seen them boots they was on the end of Bo Taylor's legs. How come you're wearing them, Tripp?"

"Well, darlin', they're mine now. Won 'em fair 'n' square."

Loretta managed a sigh rather than a scream. "You got gambling money, Tripp? Cause I ain't hardly got no fingernails left."

"I had gambling money, now I got these here boots. Ain't they something? Bo Taylor paid five hundred bucks for them, and now, they're mine."

"Well maybe you can trade them in for a washing machine and a pair of work boots, Tripp? Oh, and maybe your son would appreciate something other than fried squirrel and turnip greens for supper sometime. "

"Honey, Bo Taylor won five hundred bucks in a card game and bought these boots, and I won the boots in a card game, so it's not like any money has actually been spent now, is it? Aw, come on Honey: I got three day's work next week, and the week after. Now, I'm kinda tired, so I'm going to rest a while."

He gives Loretta a hug and smacks a kiss on her resistant lips. She finishes the laundry, sets to hoeing the turnip and collard patches, feeds her old Retriever, Blue, then goes indoors to pour herself a coffee.

There he is, leaning back, five hundred dollar boots up on the table, his mouth wide open and snoring like a hog. Sweet Jesus, how did she get here? How can she get out?

She calls Patsy Taylor. Patsy's upset on account of Bo coming home penniless and barefoot this morning. Well actually, she had been upset about that, now she's more upset because she hit him over the head with her skillet, and he was out cold for nearly an hour, and she drove him to the emergency room because he was talking funny when he came round, and then she panicked and left him there, and now she's throwing some things in a bag and she doesn't know where she's going to run to. Oh, my: one husband brain-damaged, possibly short-term, one temporarily hysterical best friend, another husband wearing five hundred bucks on his feet and dumb as a fence post. Loretta feels like probably, she should take charge here.

"Listen Hon, calm down and I'll be round just as soon as I take care of things here. Pack something pretty now, but we're travelling light. Everything'll be fine."

She finds the *Benadryl* she got when Tripp Junior got all messed up with poison ivy and was scratching like a hound last summer; she packs bags for them both; she makes a fresh pot of coffee and lets a few *Benadryl* dissolve in it; she gently shakes Tripp awake.

"Okay, Sleepy Head, time you woke up and took off those fine boots. There's fresh coffee, and a beer if you want."

"Now ain't that a better way for a woman to talk to her man? I'm saying yes to both, Darlin'."

In the kitchen, Loretta pours the coffee, opens a beer and drops a couple of *Benadryl* into the bottle. All last night's Bourbon and cigars would surely mask any taste they had. It was a struggle, but between them they managed to get the boots off before Tripp passed out again. She wraps them carefully in his best shirt and takes the bags out to the truck then she and Blue climb in. She stops at the school and explains she has to take Junior to visit a sick relative. She tells Junior why they're leaving and he gives a whoop of joy and hugs Blue.

They drive to Patsy's place. Patsy's now had a couple of beers and is singing "Kerosene" like she IS Miranda Lambert. They all join in.

They pack everything into Patsy's car: it's newer and needs less gas than the truck. They don't yet know where they're going, maybe Georgetown, or Louisville: but they have five hundred dollars to start them off and none of them are afraid of hard work. What's for sure is that they won't be driving off no cliff.

ATIF

[a chapter from a novel]
by Helen Parker

Coffee Plus was unusually quiet for a Friday in August. Maybe it would liven up later. Atif took his usual table, but today he sat with his back to the window. The sight of people walking past, chatting with friends or striding purposefully left his soul grazed. Surely there was a purpose for him, too? He shouldn't be there. He no longer had money to spend on good coffee. He should really conserve what little he had left, but he didn't know where else to go.

'Penny for them?' It was Joanna, come to take his order. He hadn't even noticed her approach.

'Er, sorry? A penny…?'

Joanna laughed. 'Sorry, it's a silly expression. It's what we say when someone is deep in thought.

'Ah. I thinking of coffee – good and strong.'

'Of course, but something else, too, I suspect.' She smiled, then returned a couple of minutes later and put a mug of the café's signature black brew in front of him. He stirred it, then sipped gratefully.

'Yes, is true. I thinking about job. I need job, then maybe… You not need chef, no?'

''Fraid not, Atif.' They looked beyond the serving counter at the back of the shop, to where they could just see Laslo moving about in the kitchen. 'But you are a man of many parts. Let's see, you've been a chef, a chauffeur, a hospital porter, a horticulturalist…'

'A horti…? I sorry, my English not so…'

'A gardener.' She perched on the chair opposite him. 'Where have you tried to look for a job?'

'At job centre. Adverts in newspaper. Friends of my friends. Building site. Everywhere.'

'And you really need something close to where you're living, I guess.'

Atif looked down. 'My friends, Sharif and Nevine, they have baby soon, so need space. I look for somewhere to live.'

'Oh, Atif! Accommodation as well! I'm so sorry. I didn't realise…' The café door opened, and Joanna went to welcome the customers and take their order. As they sat down, there was a horrendous crash in the kitchen. Atif was back in the war-torn city, bombs exploding, blinding white light shot through with red, heart hammering fit to burst, brain sloshing out of control, ears ringing, buildings collapsing in on themselves like dominoes, flying debris, shards of glass, billowing clouds of choking dust obscuring vision, grit in his teeth, a sour taste in his mouth, the metallic smell of blood, followed by the rot of death. As the clouds of dust and ash cleared, the vision of shreds of jagged masonry sheared off like frayed fabric, half-rooms, obscenely naked with bedding, clothes, toys, curtains hanging out, lives revealed for all to see. Arms, legs, bodies. Children's hysterical screams, women wailing, dogs howling, men shouting, then the aftermath of quiet unbelief, the silence of death.

'Bocsànat! Sorry,' Laslo muttered, with a few expletives. The tray of stainless steel utensils that he had dropped in the doorway of the kitchen had landed on the tiled floor. Atif was under the table, his arms shielding his head, waiting for the glass of the shop-front to come crashing over him. Coffee drip-dripped off the table on to the floor beside him. Quickly he scrambled to sit on his chair and right the mug he had tipped over as he dived for cover. He looked around. The new arrivals were chatting, but Joanna, ever attentive, arrived promptly with a cloth.

'Atif? Are you…?'

'Afwan. Shukran.' The English wouldn't come. Then, 'I sorry, so sorry, spilled coffee.' Maybe she hadn't noticed, wouldn't think…

'It was Laslo. He can be so clumsy. It was just a tray. Sorry, Atif…'

What was she thinking? Why couldn't he just live life without these unwanted flashbacks, these constant unnecessary reminders of what he had lost?

Having mopped up the spill, Joanna refilled his cup and wouldn't countenance further payment. He was grateful. It gave him an excuse to sit a little longer and to recover his equilibrium. He watched passers-by over the rim of his mug. Edinburgh in the tourist season was a magnet for all except sun-seekers. Atif quickly banished a memory of Syria's unremitting summer heat.

Midday, and the café began to buzz. Kathryn, the new waitress, arrived in the shop, disappeared into the kitchen, and quickly reappeared, tying her uniform apron. She was short and plump, not at all like the previous girl – Atif tried to remember her name. English and Scottish names could be tricky. Her name escaped him, but he remembered her regal stance and serious expression, her dark hair and that flushed face when she heard she had won a castle! Confused, Atif had asked his new friend, Mike, but Mike said it was probably a pig in a poke. So the waitress had become a farmer?

As more customers filtered into the shop, Atif knew his table would be needed, so, reluctantly, he prepared to leave but as he opened the door, Joanna ran to catch up with him. 'Atif, I might have an idea. Could you please stop by as we close and I'll tell you what I'm thinking.'

PRESCIENT DANGER

by Brian Bourner

Having been brought up in a good middle-class family, by parents who wisely had the foresight to send me to a top private school rather than a dismal comprehensive, it meant I'd had the opportunity to make lots of useful contacts with good people, people with money. That greatly helped when it came to establishing myself as an independent consultant. And now I meet all kinds of people. One day I had a nine o'clock appointment.

'Come in,' I said in response to the knock on the door of my consulting room, and sat a little straighter in my hand-stitched Italian suit as a slovenly dressed chap tumbled in. It was clear he had not been looking after himself for some time.

'Good morning' I said. 'I hope you didn't have to come too far.'

'Drove half an hour on the bloody motorway,' he complained, obviously unhappy that I had required him to visit me rather than the other way around.

It turned out he had a small plastic moulding business and for some reason plastic cutlery was going out of fashion. So I wasn't surprised to find that his firm was losing money. He had finally decided he'd better seek out some professional financial and management advice, which of course I duly offered for half an hour or so before presenting my not insignificant invoice.

On his way out, as he stared incredulously at the charges, I also offered the free suggestion that he might want to have his car fully serviced.

A few days later I read that he'd died in a motorway crash. His brakes had failed and he'd ended up as the meat in a pile-up sandwich. Fortunately my invoice was fully paid from the liquidated company's assets, as I'd predicted it would be. I had not been too surprised by the crash. You see, an inner feeling, you might say second sight, told me that if he wasn't looking after himself or his business he probably wasn't looking after his car either. Failing to wash and shave and launder clothes regularly – well, they're unfortunate but don't kill you. A failed business – well at worst you go bankrupt, you're poor but you survive. But a faulty car on a motorway – that's a death trap waiting to happen. I mean, I make sure I have my Jag serviced by a mechanic almost as regularly as I have it valet cleaned.

Some people imply I have the gift of prescience; that I can see what's going to happen in the future. It's nonsense of course. I'm no Nostradamus. Mind you the amount that old Nostradamus drank I probably could have predicted gout would get him in the end. I'm no Brahan Seer either. Just as well really, since he rightly predicted all sorts of things would happen in the future but failed to envisage that he himself would end up being burnt alive in a spiked tar barrel.

For relaxation I read detective stories and watch police dramas on TV. The protagonists are constantly invested with the ability to develop accurate 'hunches' out of thin air. It seems to me it's usually when the writers have realized there's a missing link in the plots they've devised. I like my home. I like relaxing in my home. I like my cleaning lady to have all eight rooms spotless by the time I come home. But I still have to put up with neighbours.

One of my neighbours is John Smith. He's obviously hard up and he's the most boringly conformist and conventional pipsqueak I've ever met. He once said he only tries to behave that way to set an example for the disreputable crowd he calls his 'less well behaved relatives'. To him everyone he meets is a Mr, Mrs, or Miss, a lady or gentleman; kids are always 'children' and the yobs from the nearby estate are only 'high-spirited youths'. But he's a neighbour so I try not to make my low opinion of him too obvious.

One evening I was passing the time of day with him, all the while trying to avoid chuckling at his tweedy clothes, which must have been ancient well before Noah got to work on the Ark. I even avoided smiling at his Mr This the shop assistant and Mrs That the classroom helper. He was washing his bog standard car and I happily deadpanned admiration for that thoroughly unremarkable vehicle.

Another day he informed me that he planned to buy a dog, not a sensible King Charles Spaniel or Tibet Mastiff but an ordinary canine. He professed modesty, saying he did not intend it to be ostentatious in any way. And sure enough a few days later I met him on the street as he was out walking a small brown nondescript puppy.

'Good Morning' he said in passing, in that way he had where you half expected he might doff his hat.

'How's Fido?' I asked.

'Goodness gracious', he replied, 'I only just decided today. How on earth did you know what I was going to call him?'

'Oh,' I replied, straight-faced as ever, 'just a wild guess; the gift of clairvoyance I suppose.'

But at that point I saw that his nephew - rather a black sheep among his relations, clad in the urchin uniform of grey tracksuit, trainers and baseball cap - had arrived on foot to visit his uncle. He had obviously overheard our brief conversation.

'You smug snobby bastard. You taking the piss out of old Uncle John again?' he enquired rather less than politely.

'Maybe,' I suggested, 'I could offer you a few tips on the correct use of language to help you get on in your career?'

The punch knocked me to the ground.

'Didn't see that coming did you? Clairvoyant my arse. Boxing's my game pal. It don't rely much on the use of language but you need to watch out real careful for what's coming next.'

THE MUG

by John Tucker

Robert Burnet and Jimmy Swan had trained as butlers just before the war and were good friends. They both had an interest in music. Both had been called up to serve as officers' batmen in the same battalion. Jimmy played piano and Robert was a good singer. They entertained the troops in the canteen in the evening, always keeping elders' hours to allow them to return to the officers' quarters by nine o`clock to complete their duties.

There was a regimental music competition and Robert won the prize trophy of a pewter mug on which his name and battalion crest were engraved. He displayed the mug, full of beer, on top of the piano. When anyone asked 'Where is Jimmy`s mug?' Robert would say 'Have you listened to his playing? Well he`s much worse after a pint of beer!' Actually, Jimmy was teetotal but could be mischievous at times with his music. Knowing there were all kinds of Scots and Irish in the battalion he would play tunes like *The Sash*, *The Wearing of the Green*, and *There will Always be an England (as Long as Scotland's There)*, just to liven things up.

And it was during one melee that resulted from him playing such tunes that the pewter mug disappeared.

Time passed and it was long after his army days, that one winter evening Jimmy, now an old pensioner, was coming home with his shopping. He passed a charity shop and spotted in its window a pewter mug bearing his old battalion crest and Robert's name. So he went in and purchased it.

The following day he was at Robert`s door expecting a great welcome, saying "Look what I`ve found!"

"Thanks," said Robert, without much emotion. "You know, I'm on my own now Jimmy but I never get lonely. You would be amazed at the number of old soldiers, members of our old battalion who bring the mug back to me, and then we chat about the old days. So once we've had a nice chat can you take it back to the charity shop? The staff there know to put it back front centre of the window."

Later, as Jimmy trudged back to the charity shop carrying the pewter pot, he wondered whether there had really been two mugs involved.

A QUICK TRIP TO TESCO

by Gracie Rose

As the butler trudged down the road the snow began to settle all around him. It was a long walk to the village and the inn, and he had neither the energy nor the urgency to rush. He was wallowing, but then didn't he deserve to wallow at least a little? His whole world had come crashing down around him in so little time and he didn't know where he was supposed to go from here.

Forward seemed like the only option for now – forward down the road towards the inn. This was no time to look back, but even when the butler did glance over his shoulder, he found that the mansion had already disappeared from view. Hidden as the snow clouds sank lower and lower.

The inn was crowded, the whole village seemed to be gathered around the bar, drinking their troubles away. In the grate, a fire roared. It was warm inside, from the heat of the flames and the bodies, and all of the windows had steamed up, a stark contrast to the snow. He lamented his sorry situation. The inn was cheery enough, but it was crowded, and sludge had been trailed in from the outside on the boots of the patrons. He didn't want to be here. He wanted to be back in the mansion – in that beautiful house that he often imagined could be his, at least when no-one else was around. But it wasn't his. That had been made abundantly clear. It wasn't his, and now it wasn't even his home anymore either. What was he to do now? He had worked for that family all his life; he was too old to be looking for something new. He had gotten too used to the way things were. That always seems to be the way, doesn't it? The moment you get too comfortable, the rug is swept out from under you.

It wouldn't do much good dwelling on it tonight though. There was nothing he could do about it now – and with the blizzard picking up outside, there was nowhere else to go either. For now, he might as well join all the other patrons in drinking his troubles away.

He picked up the pewter mug that the innkeeper handed him and drained its contents in as few swigs as he could manage. Then instantly regretted it. The ale wasn't particularly strong, but he was not a practised drinker, and it went straight to his head. He grimaced, pressing his eyes shut as the world began to tilt dizzyingly on its axis. He knew he was not a practised drinker, but still he was surprised by how quickly the feeling overtook him. Surely, he couldn't have gotten drunk that quickly?

When he opened his eyes again, the light was much brighter – a cold, hard white had replaced the orange glow of the inn. As he took in his surroundings, such a shock came over him, that he staggered backwards. The pewter mug slipped from his grasp and clattered to the ground.

The lights overhead were bright white and built into the ceiling. They flickered and hissed every so often like lightning trapped in a tube. They were so bright they hurt his eyes and he had to look away. He stood in a wide aisle and on either side of him, there were shelves stacked high with smooth, shiny packets. It was cold in the aisle, like the freezing snow outside. He peered into the shelves, lit with that same strange light, and saw that the smooth shiny packages held food. Meat, fish, cheese, and butter, all arranged neatly – a feast of such variety as he had never seen, all wrapped up and sealed. Strange music was echoing from somewhere above his head, some trick of the panelled ceiling that threw the sound around. He didn't know what to make of any of it. Someone must have slipped something stronger into his ale. He thought he must be hallucinating but even his imagination could not surely invent such a strange and alien world. He didn't have the creativity for such a feat.

There were a few people in the narrow aisle, and he

considered approaching one of them demanding to know where he was, but they were such strange looking folk that he doubted they would even be able to understand one another. He was still getting his bearings (or more rightly, failing to) when a voice from behind him made him turn.

"This yours, mate?" asked a tall and rather scruffy gentleman (though gentleman was not quite the right word). He was wearing a blue polo shirt with the word 'Tesco' printed across its breast. The butler watched as he reached down to retrieve the pewter mug, but the moment he gripped its handle, both he and it disappeared. And the butler found himself staring dumbstruck at the gap where the man had stood, entirely unsure of where he was supposed to go from there.

A few of the patrons in the inn turned their heads when the man in the blue polo shirt suddenly appeared on the bar stool, looking startled and disoriented, but most of them took no notice. It was crowded in the inn, and they were too drunk to mind the odd hapless time traveller who stumbled into their midst.

DO NOT DISTURB

by Stéphanie Voytier

Nathalie opened her eyes slowly. A thin beam of light shone through the gap in the shutters. It was bright and warm and she knew it was a sunny day. The sound of chirping birds reached her sleepy mind and she smiled. That was a treat, a Sunday treat. The rest of the week, Paris got up far too early and the traffic muffled the joyful morning chorus. She yawned lazily and looked at the alarm clock on the bedside table. 07:46. Good, it was the perfect time to go to the market. Her stomach rumbled as she realised how ravenous she was and a sudden vision of her Sunday breakfast flashed in her mind.

Croissant, pain au chocolat, cafe noir. At this time of the day, her favourite table at La Brasserie St Ouen would be free.

She jumped out of bed and made a mental list of the things she needed to buy while she dressed. Tulips were at the top. She wanted to join the birds in their spring celebration. A few minutes later, she was walking down rue Lamark, humming a song and pulling her shopping trolley behind her. As she reached the bottom of the street, she noticed the colourful leaflet taped on the window of the wool shop and stopped.

'Audition for La compagnie du Train Bleu.
Want to join a young but creative theatre company?
Come and meet us on Wednesday 6th May, 7.30pm'
Nathalie knew it by heart. She had even checked the address to see if she could go after work. But it was silly, of course. She wouldn't go. Her parents had been right to discourage her from going to a drama school. At thirty, her life was nicely sorted with a good job and a more than decent wage. She ignored her clenched stomach and resumed her walk.

Like every Sunday, the local shops had set up their stalls on the narrow pavement and Nathalie dived with relish into the colours, the smells and the joyous hustle-bustle. Mrs Germain, the florist, was her first stop. She bought two bouquets and left them behind, planning to pick them up on her way back. Then she went to see Aziz, the owner of the small Moroccan delicatessen packed with spices, fresh pastries and exotic fruits. As usual, he slipped two peaches in her trolley as he handed her the bill. 'A little gift for my favourite client!' Her visit to the cheesemonger was the longest. George wanted her to taste a new blue cheese and she spent time choosing her weekly selection. And then... Then came the anomaly. Between George's shop and Damien's, the butcher, there was a gap. And this gap had remained a mystery since she moved into the area, three years before.

A narrow door took the space between the two shops. Its glass panels were so dirty that it was impossible to see what was inside. A notice was tucked in the corner near the door handle. It said 'Do not disturb'. There was nothing strange about it but what was intriguing was the reaction of the shopkeepers when Nathalie enquired about the door. A shrug, a cryptic smile and a quick change of conversation. Even the concierge of her building, usually so talkative and helpful, refused to tell her. And so what had been a trivial enquiry had become a real mystery.

That Sunday morning, when she left George and passed in front of the door, she gave a quick glance as usual and her heart skipped a bit. The door was ajar. She continued to walk mechanically and then stopped. She turned round and looked again. Yes, the door was opened. She retraced her steps and came closer to it. She looked around but no one was paying attention to her. On an impulse, she pushed the door and stepped in. A strong smell of incense enveloped her. A long corridor stretched ahead of her, its floor covered with leaflets, its walls dirty and bare. At the end of it, there was another door. It was ajar too and she could see a bright light through the opening. She parked her trolley against the wall and walked silently to the door. Should she knock? Should she push the door discreetly and peer inside? What would she find? But she didn't need to do anything. The door suddenly opened wide and she stood face to face with a small man.

'I was expecting you' he said with a kind smile, 'please, come in.'

Nathalie was stunned. Expected? The man moved aside to let her in and encouraged her with a nod. She was hesitant. She could hear her mum say, 'Don't follow strangers Nathalie, and don't talk to people you don't know.' But she wasn't a baby anymore, was she? And she had a good feeling about the man. The deep lines around his dark eyes gave him a cheery look. He closed the door as she stepped in and he invited her to sit down. He sat in the armchair opposite hers and waited patiently as she looked around. She liked the room at once. The carved wooden table standing between them, the colourful rug, the cushions on the wee sofa against the wall, the hookah, the ivory paintings on the wall, everything reminded her of her visits to India, Burma and Pakistan.

When her eyes finally met his, he said, 'Shall we start?'

He picked up a set of tarot cards from a stool on his side and spread them on the table, their backs facing upwards.

'Pick up three cards please,' he said.

Nathalie wanted to laugh. What was this all about? He wasn't serious, surely, he didn't expect her to hold with such nonsense. But something in the eyes of the man startled her. The cheery look had vanished and he was observing her with a steady gaze.

Nathalie picked up three cards and turned them.

'Three more,' asked the man and she obeyed.

He looked at the cards and said, 'Something happened today.'

'No, nothing special happened,' said Nathalie, shaking her head. She shrugged, almost apologetic.

'Tell me exactly what you did this morning since you got up, please.'

Slightly embarrassed, Nathalie began to tell him.

'Stop!' he interrupted suddenly, Tell me more about the ad in the wool shop.'

Her stomach lurched and she frowned,

'It was just an ad about a theatre company!' she said on the defensive. .

'Why is it so important to you?' he insisted.

'I never said it was important!'

'You wanted to be an actress?' he asked with a sudden softness in his voice.

'Are you kidding?' she thought with anger, 'Is it all you can do? Every little girl wants to be an actress!' But she didn't say anything and simply nodded.

'What stopped you?'

'My parents.' And she felt tears fill her eyes.

He continued to look at her, as if she ought to guess his next question.

'Are your parents still holding the rudder? Or are you a grown-up now?' he finally asked.

His questions were like a slap on her face. How dare he! She wasn't a baby any more, of course she was in charge of her own life. She was a dependable woman. She was a successful executive in a big insurance company. She was... she was... And then something broke in her, like a dam suddenly giving way. Tears began to flood down her cheeks and an immense sense of relief engulfed her. Of course she was in charge of her life. Of course she would go to the audition.

'Thank you,' she said as she got up, 'how much do I owe you?'

'Nothing, but I'd like to know how you are getting on.'

'How do I get in touch with you?' she asked with a shaky voice.

'The door is always unlocked. And don't mind the notice, you'll always come at the right time.'

A PEA-SOUPER

by Helen Parker

'A fog lamp - a flash-light - a flaming torch!'

'What?' Greg asked.

Laura stood at the window looking at the fog. Londoners would've called it a pea-souper. No work during lockdown had been bad enough, but redundancy was infinitely worse. 'The fog. It's so dense, I can't see where I'm going. I need a light.'

'But we're not going out anywhere, and it'll have blown over by tomorrow.'

She sighed. 'I don't mean that sort of fog.'

Greg pushed the laptop back and frowned, trying to understand.

This is my life!' she wailed. 'I can't see where I'm going.'

'I'm good-looking and sexy and you can see *me*.'

That raised the ghost of a smile, but then Hannah-next-door appeared in her garden with a bunch of pink balloons.

'What's Hannah doing?' Greg said, joining Laura at the window.

'It's Poppy's first birthday. They're having a party for her. Look, Andrew's blowing up more balloons.'

They could see their neighbour in his front room, a curly-haired blonde toddler clinging to his trouser leg, while Hannah fixed the first bunch on the gate post.

Ours wouldn't be blonde, Laura thought. *It would be a boy - he'd have black hair and appealing dark puppy-dog eyes like Greg's...if only...* Greg always knew what she was thinking. His hug heralded her tears. 'If only we could...'

'Give it time,' he urged. 'It's not the same for everyone. It's just taking longer for us. And now that you're not out at work, you might be more relaxed, and...'

'But redundancy's so dehumanising. And going out to work used to distract me from... from other things.' She pulled out of his hug and turned away from the window. 'The very word, redundancy. It means not needed. Surplus to requirements.'

'Not to me, you're not. To me, you're the absolutely essential one-and-only.'

'Flattery will get you everywhere!' She smiled despite the tears and planted a kiss on his cheek.

After a pause, he continued, 'But you weren't the only one to get the push.'

'No, but the other two took *voluntary* redundancy. They were putting the flags out, delighted.

'You could just stay home. Be a lady of leisure.'

'I *am*. What choice do I have?'

'No, I mean - *choose* to stay home. I earn enough for us both.'

'It's not just money. I'd stay home if...'

'I know.'

Back at the window, she couldn't settle. Even her brain was a fog.

'Well, why don't you take a university course?'

'I'm already a graduate.'

'Take another course.'

'Like what?'

'An Education certificate. You could teach home economics.'

'You mean, show *other* people how to stay at home?'

The fog outside was thickening. It was like milk, like curds and whey. Like semolina, like pea soup... She clapped a hand over her mouth and rushed for the bathroom.

Greg banged on the door. 'What is it?'

Eventually, she emerged. Triumphantly, she held up the stick with the little blue line.

'A fog lamp - a flash-light - a flaming torch!'

THE GARDEN PATH

by Brian Bourner

"I've told you this story before of course, but I suppose it's always quite entertaining. So, since you insist, I don't mind telling it again.

"It was a Saturday morning in May, made me a bit uncomfortable being unseasonably warm and my wife Kirstie was outside weeding our small garden. She was quite a card Kirstie. She always took it to enormous lengths – all sorts of pots, rakes, shovels, shears, and trellis for plants to climb up and so on. People passing always smiled to see all this equipment on the little path in our tiny front garden. She always found money for gardening from somewhere – it seemed to me she was always finding money for seeds, canes, etc. etc. rather than more important things. And I was up about half eleven and it was Cup Final day so I was checking to see there was plenty of beer and crisps in the cupboard when I heard her shouting 'Could you come and help me re-pot some of these plants George?' She was a real card. As if I'd want to be out grubbing around in the muck on my day off and the Cup Final coming up soon on the TV. So of course I shouted back that I was busy. And then searching around did I not find we were out of beer. All the money must have been wasted on gardening tools. Or else someone must have drunk it. Isn't it funny how your mind works? That was when I remembered I'd been having a bit of a session with Lenny the night before and he only left about three when the beer ran out, and that maybe explained why my mind was a bit blurry.

Hangovers aren't so bad you know, all you ever need is a hair of the dog. 'We need more beer,' I shouted. I was a bit angry that she'd let us run out. She was always up for a laugh Kirstie. 'Just help me with these pots first,' she called back 'and then I'll run round quick to the shop for more beer." So of course I went out into the little front garden to make the point quite strongly that it would be much better if she went for the beer first. But she was in that jokey mood of hers and said 'Surely the beer can wait a bit? Help me lift this pot first.' That was when I took hold of her shoulders, just to give her a bit of a shake and help her come to her senses and stop her joking around. But she looked at me like I was some kind of wild hairy monster and before I knew it my hands had slipped round her neck. It's funny how these things can happen. I think she was throttled a bit. It was an accident. It's funny how these things can happen. I let go but still being a bit wobbly I staggered backwards and tripped over a spade. And blow me if it wasn't a new spade I'd never seen before. I was so annoyed by it, tripping me up and all, that I grabbed the stupid thing and hurled it out of the way. Just by chance it somehow must have reached the little garden path and landed on Kirstie. What a pantomime, eh?"

"The spade landed on your wife?"

"That's it."

"And she was found half-strangled with a spade embedded in her upper body."

"Well that's what they said. It's funny how these things can happen, isn't it?"

"Not really. Parole application refused."

DANGEROUS MAGIC

by Georgina Tibai

'I found it!' With difficulty, Mary pulled the heavy, leather-bound book out of an old, ornate chest. Her small hands were trembling slightly with the weight of it as she proudly presented the find to her mother. 'Look, it's red and has the crest, just as you said!'

'Well done, pumpkin!' Her mother smiled and took the hefty book from the little girl. She opened it and showed Mary the first page.

'That's the one! See, here it says. Property of Mary Elizabeth McGowan.' She pointed at a curvaceous, handwritten line.

Mary couldn't read it yet, but she thought it was beautiful. She ran her fingers through the letters. 'She really was named after you, mom?'

Mary Elizabeth laughed. 'I was named after her. See, here?' She tapped her finger on a small, elaborate sign. 'This is her warding spell. It was the first spell I learned. It would blind anyone who tried to read this book without permission.'

Mary stepped back instantly. Her mother closed the book and stroked her head. 'Good instinct. But we are direct descendants. You are safe. We need to make sure we give permission to your dad, though! Magic is a dangerous tool. You need to know what you are doing because the consequences can be devastating - that means terrible.'

Mary's face lit up. 'Like the Gruffalo?'

Her mother laughed again. 'Yes, pumpkin, quite so. Shall we get ourselves a nice cup of hot chocolate for the story?'

The lounge was basking in the golden hue of the late afternoon sunshine. Mother and daughter sat curled up in a cosy armchair by the window, steaming cups in hand. Mary Elizabeth looked at her girl with a serious expression.

'It is not a tale for the faint-hearted, pumpkin. Are you sure you are ready?'

She nodded with a severe face which utterly failed to hide her excitement. Her mother put down her cup on the side table and picked up the book. She perused the pages for a while, and then stopped at a picture of a man and a horse. The man had a menacing glare. The horse was big and black with strange, sharp-looking teeth. Mary Elizabeth smiled at her daughter and cleared her throat.

'My encounter with the creature known as the Kelpie, as it was detailed in my diary -

9th September 1916: Gavin, the butcher's boy, didn't go home yesterday. Sarah, his mother, rallied a search but to no avail. This morning they found his flute near the riverbank. The rains were heavy lately, and the river swelled up. The people fear the worst. What a terrible tragedy in the midst of all we must endure. I went to see Sarah. She cannot believe it. She keeps saying what a swimmer her boy was. But the current is cruel. All children are forbidden to go near the water.

24th September 1916: Little Rosie vanished. She was supposed to meet her mother near the jetty to help with the fish. It would have been her first time. Two children in two weeks, it makes the people scared. They are pointing fingers already. Poor Malcolm, the war invalid, is getting dirty looks. He was sent home with terrible head injuries and has been odd since, but that's no reason to hate. I never liked him much, but at least I have the decency to be ashamed of it now. I must do something. I feel there is a new presence in town. Someone who decided not to proclaim themselves. I must investigate.

30th September 1916: Our new resident is a Kelpie, I am sure of it. I couldn't find him yet, but he leaves a distinct magical residue on the river bank. Maybe because of his shape-shifting? If I am right, he must be stopped. I am working on a spell, but I need a full moon to finish it.

6th October 1916: Another one. I wish I had a better, quicker way! Poor Lily, her poor mother! I cannot forgive myself. I went out tonight with a firearm and a warding charm, but the monster didn't show. Only a few days till the full moon. I hope tragedy won't strike again.

7th October 1916: 1 failed. I couldn't save Lily, and I couldn't save Malcolm. A mob marched to his house, and a fire broke out. The house burned down with him in it. Alive or dead, we will never know. The authorities decided it was an accident. Now everyone seems to think they are safe. I will have to put an end to this.

11th October 1916: Tonight. I am ready. I left a note to my John in case the containment circle fails to work. I will summon the creature and kill him.

12th October 1916: I couldn't destroy the beast, but at least it will not harm more innocents. I summoned him to the well in my garden. When it rose from it, I shot him, but that only angered the creature who then tried to attack me. My circle held, and the entire clip seemed to have an effect. The Kelpie tried to escape through the water, but my circle prevented that too. Short of other options, I decided to bind him to the well. I will have to find a way to silence him too. He is pleading now, trying to convince me he knows nothing of the murders.

13th October 1916: Finally, some peace. I boarded up the well.

9th November 1916: There have been no more disappearances. Tonight, at the full moon, I will reinforce the bind and hopefully bind his tongue as well. It feels good to have been able to do my part. To keep my people safe from the beast.'

The afternoon gold in the room was turning into twilight orange. Mary Elizabeth closed the book and looked at her daughter. She looked back at her with wild eyes.

'We have a Kelpie in grandma's garden?!'

Mary Elizabeth raised her eyebrows.

'Not exactly the reaction you were waiting for, love?' A male voice carried into the room, and a tall, ginger man followed. 'Our little adventuress - '

Mary's voice cut in sharply. 'You have our permission to read the book, dad!'

Duncan looked amused. 'What's that, my darling?'

'Not exactly the reaction you were waiting for, love?' Mary Elizabeth looked smug.

Duncan snorted. 'I guess we just have to reinforce that the old-fashioned way.' He crouched down in front of his daughter. 'Darling, you have to promise mom and dad that you will keep away from the old well. It is dangerous in more ways than one, and we need to know that you won't go near it. Promise?'

The little girl frowned and looked from one parent to another. They returned her gaze as a united front, and she relented. 'Okay, I promise.'

They beamed at her. 'Thank you, pumpkin. How about we go and pick some evening stock? I can smell them from here.'

She squealed. 'I'll get the basket!' And she ran out of the room.

'We should just blow up that well. I don't like her being near it.' Duncan couldn't keep the worry out of his voice this time. 'We have been over this. We don't know if that killed the creature or freed it.'

'She will be fine. I grew up here, remember?' Mary Elizabeth stood up, and Duncan pulled her into his embrace. They stood there for a moment until a shriek came from the kitchen.

'Mom, granny's back!'

They walked out of the room hand in hand. The book was forgotten, gleaming in the late sunlight.

A FLIGHT OF FANCY

by Brian Bourner

"Chorying gear from Wilson's shed? It's not your brightest idea Askew." I kept trying to tell him but his money worries were so bad he was already talking of topping himself. Wilson's stack of nicked gear was the only thing preventing it, what Askew saw as his only hope. He said he could break in and sell some of the iPhones to pay off the loan sharks who were hunting him down.

I'd only known Iain a short time, long enough to know he always went by his surname, Askew. I'd recently been posted to Edinburgh to assist with work on a transport bypass, an intersection having problems with hitchhikers. I found the cost of living prohibitive. The accommodation allowance I'd been allocated was not too generous so I'd ended up living in Muirhouse. That was where we met. He was my neighbour and we'd become friends. He didn't mind that my hunchback made me look a little deformed, or that I was pale enough to seem almost translucent. It impressed him as an extreme scheme tan. I'd met Maggie, the girl he lived with, and their two small daughters. They were the epitome of the 'just barely managing' family.

"He's got that shed wired with a security system," I reminded him. "If that alarm goes off…" but Askew had the bit between his teeth and desperation was making him determined.

"Makes it easier," he interrupted, insisting "Any numptie with bulging biceps and bolt cutters can get past shed locks and chains. Even a specimen like you could hide bolt cutters under that old coat you're always wearing. But chopping up padlocks? Leaves behind clear evidence of a break-in. Now with an electronic security system all you need is the passcode. Then you just open the door, walk in, take what you want, close the door again and nobody's any the wiser, especially not Mad-Dog Wilson."

"At least until he's checking his stock again before moving it on to his fence. And how do you get the code anyway?"

"I've already got it. Wilson doesn't generally let the guys doing the nicking anywhere near his shed. But I knocked a phone last week and when I delivered it he already had a laptop and an X-Box to put away so he let me give him a hand. He might be built like a brick shit-house but he's still only got two hands. I just watched over his shoulder. See, I'm only taking back stuff he forced me to nick anyway."

"How 'forced' Askew?"

"Ok, I admit I agreed the first time because I thought he'd share the ill-gotten gains. But he didn't. Nuthin. Nae pochle. Empty sky rocket."

"So why go on thieving for this twenty-first century Fagin if you're getting absolutely nothing out of it?"

"Threatened to mark Maggie and the bairns if I didn't keep at it. He means it. He's a bad bastard, a total claw hammer, more Voldemort than Malfoy, well out of order. He was running with the Young Pilton team before he could walk. He's been in tight with a lot of heavies ever since, most of them in Saughton or the Bar-L now but some still on the street. Once he's got you on the hook getting out isn't so easy Tam, believe me. Ye ken how it is."

I took a minute to meditate on the situation. Askew was only stealing because of intimidation, because of Wilson's evil threats. But even if Wilson didn't actually catch him breaking into his shed it still wouldn't take him long to discover stuff was missing. He'd put two and two together. Then Askew would probably wish he's just topped himself.

I looked into Askew's desperate eyes.

"Listen," I said quietly. "Let me do the job. I'll break in tonight, grab some phones, knock them out to punters round the boozers tomorrow. Then I'll bring you the readies."

"Great if you'd do that Tam. Mind, he'd still hear about it quick enough. And when he asks around, the punters in any of the howffs round here won't be slow to mark your card. Besides, with your wee thin body and hump back, you might struggle to do the job, and why would you really want to do it anyway?"

"Cuz you're my china Askew. Just give me the code and leave everything to me. And maybe get yourself a good alibi for tonight in case Wilson comes knocking on your door later."

So I did the job that night, in and out quick, sold the gear the following day. Tired after trekking round boozers and gassing with ne'er-do-weels I was sitting on my own on a park bench come the evening and contemplating a good day's work. That was when I looked up and saw Wilson's size twelves tramping purposefully across the grass, his beady eyes fixed on me. Something glinted in his hand. Stress shot up through my spine to my brain. Fight or flight. The amygdala had me on my feet and already moving backwards, but the hippocampus was still in there pitching, arguing that sensible debate might still win the day, though maybe after a small altercation with hopefully not too much blood spilled.

Then Wilson was right in my face.

"Your tea's oot Tam. Gadgies in the German cruiser grassed ye up. Yer a bastard tea leaf."

Just like Askew, I thought. Pot kettle.

"And that wee shit Askew was in on it, wasn't he? Think I'm glaekit? No way you just hacked the shed's security code. He'll get what's coming anaw. What's for him will certainly no' go by him - or his bairns, or their ma neither."

Wilson gripped the handle of the blade, his knuckles white and his arm starting to swing. I could see the rational argument approach wasn't going to work as well as the hippocampus might have hoped, and that I'd also made a few logical errors when it came to notions of shifting blame and responsibility. I leapt backwards, throwing off my coat just as the blade whizzed past my face. Wilson's eyes bulged seeing me suddenly naked, my thin pale white body.

"Right, you're potted heid pal."

His fist started swinging again. But I instantly spread the wings that make up the hump in my back and hovered above him. The blade flashed through empty space again while I remembered it's a wonderful life.

"What the fuck?" inquired my puzzled tormentor as he peered up at my feet, his mouth hanging open. "You a fuckin ghost or something?"

"Well yes, the flying is a bit unusual," I agreed. Fluttering above him I tried to explain. "There are more things in heaven and earth Horatio…"

"The fuck's Horatio?"

"….supernatural things… sprites, fairies, harpies, angels – all three triads of them - and fifth dimension beings… parallel universes…..wings really aren't that unusual……"

But I could see I'd lost him. I wasn't getting through. I decided against discussing the laws of quantum mechanics, time shifts and simultaneous existence in multiple places. So as he stared up, vacant and wordless, I reluctantly said "Ok, we'll do it the old-fashioned way Wilson."

Physical strength is another one of those attributes those appraising us find it hard to believe we possess; at least not until they're being hauled through the sky like that boy hanging on to the snowman, but screaming instead of laughing. I kicked the knife out of his hand, gripped his arm, and jerked him off the ground.

I deposited Wilson in the Upper Amazon jungle. If the indigenous tribes let him live I imagine, given his skill with cutting tools, they'll probably chuck him out soon so he can try throwing in his lot with other destructive types intent on destroying this planet's greenery. Just as well this isn't the only planet in the universe.

When I eventually saw Askew again I passed him the money and stressed he'd better steer clear of illegal activity in future. He remarked that luckily he hadn't seen Wilson for a while. I said I'd heard he went travelling and the Bogeyman got him.

"Ya dancer" he murmured and a relieved smile crossed his face. I think he interpreted my comment as an allusion to arrest and imprisonment. He said he regretted his past criminal activity. "Well that's it for me and chorying Tam. Never again."

"By the way," I said. "I think it would be a good idea if you made an anonymous phone call and let the police know about the stuff still in the shed. They can arrange to return items to their rightful owners."

Askew scowled at this suggestion. "Aye, well maybe I will," he muttered in a reluctant tone that sounded not quite scoffing but a little less than fully committed. But I suppose you just have to have faith in other life forms sometimes.

"And I'm sorry," I said, "you won't see me around for a while. My firm want me on this other job that's come up. It's quite far away, in fact its worlds away from this place."

"Ach that's a shame Tam. Ye've been a pal. But maybe it'll no be so far away that ye find yersel doon amang the Sassenachs."

"No," I said, "I don't think I'll be heading south. Onwards and upwards, eh?"

"Gie my door a knock when you get back Tam."

"Sure Iain, I mean Askew."

Iain Askew, I mean, I ask you.

A CHILDHOOD
(A Subconscious Dream Never Realised)

by Ian Elliot

Foreword *(for an autobiography)*:

It was the last Christmas we had on the farm, the year of 1967. Both my brother, Drew, and I had lived with our Mum (Lily), and Dad (John), at Easter Cowden Farm by Dalkeith for twelve years or so. Drew was eighteen and I was just turning fourteen. We moved away in the spring of 1968.

I was two years old when we had moved to this farm from Fordel Mains, near Pathhead, the place where I was born in 1954, in the little cottage closest to the farmyard and outbuildings.

That Christmas and New Year were as normal as any of the others we had enjoyed. I guess our parents had already started to make moves about not just moving house but making a whole new life away from farming. Dad was forty-five and Mum was forty years of age.

Christmas Day was full of presents to open and food to be eaten, but in those years public holidays were few and far between. Dad could only take either Christmas Day or New Year's Day as a holiday. He chose the latter as it guaranteed there would be a party somewhere to bring in the New Year. And who could blame him; a bottle of whisky in those days was a real luxury and it was guaranteed to be finished within a day or two of the New Year.

He may not have been with us for most of Christmas Day but Dad always made it to the Christmas Dinner table and all of us caught up with him as regards our presents and to give him his. Thankfully that was his working day over when the Christmas Dinner hit the table.

My main present that year was an electronics kit made by Philips. It consisted of components that allowed for various battery-operated electronic devices to be constructed and dismantled in order to make items such as an automatic night-time switch to turn on a lamp, a moisture detector for pot plants, and a medium wave AM radio receiver complete with earpiece and internal antenna for receiving the signal. I remember a Morse code Generator as well.

Little did I know at the time that this electronics kit was really a boxful of destiny. It changed my life completely, leading me to venture into the Radio/Television and Electronics Industry for the next fifty odd years - right up until I retired in 2019.

THE COUNTRYMAN

by Robin King

He was someone I knew to a fair degree as most years Family and I visited him. It was a visit we all looked forward to. After many long years I am trying to describe how I saw him as a person who worked hard, led a simple country life, loved nature and his God.

He worked his smallholding of fifteen acres placed in rural Wigtownshire. He had left school at fourteen years of age to work in the pits to earn only for the household. He was now where he was due to the commands of his father - HE decided what was to be done and no one else.

The smallholding was set up at the foot of the knoll, the top of which gave views of the lush, rolling farmlands spreading a carpet of deep grass upon which were splashes of black and white cattle grazing contentedly in what seemed like everlasting sunshine. The vibrant humming of insects going about their business filled the air and the scent of clover was present. In the distance the sea shimmered and glistened in the sunshine, tinted with the faintest touch of sea mist. From time to time the cattle made the sounds expected of them despite the heat.

The small Byre by the house had four stalls, each enclosing a cow waiting to be milked. They were content. The walls of the Byre were spotlessly whitewashed and overhead a bright red iron clad roof was supported by thick hornbeam rafters. The four inset windows let in shafts of penetrating light which highlighted the animals. The red door, ajar, gave passage to the darting swallows as they fetched and carried to feed their young in the mud coated nests clinging to the walls and beams.

The man was stocky - no more than five feet tall. He had high cheek bones, cherry red cheeks streaked with veins and a strong roman nose also streaked. His eyes of palest blue sparkled under strong eyebrows. They displayed a sense of mischief but also a deep thoughtful soul. His strong teeth were purest white and he was capped by a mass of strong, dark brown hair. He was a man who had worked hard but lived a good, simple country life.

As he milked each cow in turn, he sang with the richness comparable to that of the greatest Tenor, the sound, reverberating around the walls and roof and out through the door into the fields beyond. All of nature loved what it heard. The man had his voice, his home, his fields, his cows and above all, his God. He had need of very little else.

The Countryman was happy - very happy. Those who knew him were happy in his presence. Man and nature were as one.

All was contentment.

INTUITION CAN ONLY TAKE YOU SO FAR

by Gracie Rose

We sit at the kitchen table, the glow of the bulb above us is such a bright white that it is starting to give me a headache. All of this is starting to give me a headache. I absently scratch my stubble. I don't know how long we can go on like this.

She sits with her head in her hands now, to hide her face, to hide the hurt that I would always be able to see. Before she had brushed it off, but even then, I could see right through her guise. I always could tell when there was something wrong. I suppose you could call it intuition. From the way that she had been sitting, I could tell that she was not alright, even as she told me that she was. From the way that she said it, I could tell that she didn't want to talk about it.

Well, that's not strictly true – she just didn't want to talk to me.

She was obviously desperate to talk about it – it was eating away at her inside and if she stayed silent much longer, she would end up hollow – she just didn't want to talk to me. She does not trust me with whatever weight it is she carries. I would never be enough for her. I had always been able to tell, and I am beginning to tire of the knowledge of it. I don't know how long we can go on like this.

If she can't tell me what was wrong, how can we ever move past it? Intuition can only take you so far.

* * *

He thinks he knows exactly what I am thinking, I can see it in the shimmer of hurt in his eyes, but intuition can only take you so far. He doesn't know, not really.

This always happens. It's always late in the kitchen under the glow of the too-bright light when we should have been asleep hours ago. He asks questions I don't have the answers for yet and he doesn't see how hard I am trying to find them. He doesn't understand why I can't seem to close this distance.

If he could spend just a moment in my mind, he would understand how badly I want to talk to him – to tell him everything. If I could share this weight with him, then perhaps my shoulders would not tense up every time that he touches my hand. But he doesn't understand my silence.

He doesn't see that it is a compliment, really. Wherever I found quiet I would always fill it with white noise – if I didn't then the sound of nothing would press in on my eardrums until it hurt – but with him I am beginning to grow bold. With him, I can edge closer to that precipice. I can lean over it and look down at all these unspoken things without fearing I might fall.

With him, I think that maybe if I let this silence between us grow, if he is patient enough, one day there may be room enough amongst the quiet for me to find the words I so desperately need. Words I could voice only to him. Maybe then he will understand. Maybe then we will finally close this distance.

Maybe... but I am beginning to doubt it.

I can tell that he is losing patience. I suppose you could call it intuition, but I have a feeling that when I finally find my voice, his ears will be long gone.

THE FUNERAL

by Robin King

The moon was in its third phase. It had been raining on the night of the new moon, which augured badly for this particular phase. The constant pounding of the rain had reduced the peat to black, oozing mud. The common grazings struggled to maintain the weight of the animals. The township sheep huddled behind whatever shelter there was; houses, sheds, peat stacks, old cars - anything that might give shelter from the remorseless wind and rain.

  The Croft house stood at the end of a grey gravel track, lined on either side by a three strand fence, ending with a cattle grid. The house was of a basic design, four windows to the front - two downstairs and two upstairs - which was repeated at the rear. It was roofed with black tiles of slate with a chimney stack at each end from which protruded two chimney pots. Thick peat smoke was being torn from the pots by the gale force wind. The outside walls were of Barra Haarl. The lights from the house struggled to be seen through the curtain of rain.

  As the first of the mourners reached the dark green door, the track and the weather having tested their determination to reach it, they were solemnly welcomed. Their coats were taken, then they were ushered into the living room. The room was warm and filled with the aroma of peat smoke and four rows of assorted wooden chairs were laid out for seating.

  They sat there in singular silence. The clocks were stopped and any mirrors or pictures had their faces turned to the wall. Each person arriving was given a stiff nod of acknowledgement from those assembled. Soon the chairs were all occupied.

The minister arrived, dressed all in black save for his white collar. He stood before the gathering, said a prayer, then some words about the deceased, and then the precentor led the singing of the hymns. A further prayer, then silence as people walked around the coffin in final reverence of the deceased. The grey dawn streaked across the sky. It continued to rain.

The graveyard lay on a rock-strewn hillside overlooking the sea, which lay open to the south-westerly gale. Some gulls still had the tenacity to fly and screech despite the wind. The sea had been whipped up to a luminous green against a black sky. White-crested waves battered the shoreline forming a long line of bubbling froth. The hillside boulders had a ghostly-white tinge which contrasted sharply against the black peat.

The land decreed that each grave could only have one layer. The man in black said the last rites which were barely audible above the wind. Eight men lowered the coffin into the shallow grave which was filling fast with water. Two men hastily filled the grave with earth, displacing the water as they did so. As everyone left for home, pools of surface water were gathering around the graveside.

The grave was left to the elements. The body to God.

There were no flowers, no tears, no emotions - only silence and solemnity. The grief would come later.

The man had lived a hard life as a crofter-fisherman. He had known what it was to handbait yards of fishing line, to row an open boat into the winds of the Atlantic Ocean. To lay the lines, to haul them in, followed by the long hard row home with the catch. To cut peats, to gather and shear the sheep and to scythe the corn. Some years were good , with some money to spare, others ended in debt. He had raised six children and despite the harshness of his life there had been many good times. There was always food - simple but wholesome. In winter there were songs and stories around the peat fire and in the long days of summer - the cutting and stacking of the peat for the next winter ahead. The joy of birth, the worry of illness, the coming together of the community in birth, death, marriage and other ceremonies. the clipping of the sheep and the singing and the dancing, - a fast disappearing life.

The man feared God.

At his burial the elements had remained ferocious. He however had entered a world of peace and everlasting life. His family would miss him but he had gone to join his wife who had died six years earlier. The durability of the man's faith had equalled that of the rocks on the land which had formed such a large part of his life.

The grieving would last seven days, during which time the wind never let up - testing the people and the land. Many of the mourners were never seen or heard of again.

MEMORIES OF MY GRANDPARENTS

by Valentina Romanazzi

Wikipedia defines memory as the retention of information over time for the purpose of influencing future action. As I became an adult, the memories I hold dearest have been replaced and exchanged as my understanding of my grandmother and her impact on my life has grown.

When I was a kid I never understood her stopping to take a purposeful moment and admire the flowers. Now that I'm grown up, I too see the beauty she saw in nature and relate to her in a way I never could as a child. As I travel the world and immerse myself in each new culture, I finally understand her fascination with visiting churches. I am far from the twelve year old that groaned at each church on our then-sightseeing itinerary.

Of course, the memories I cherished as a child are even more special today. From the smell of "ragu" on Sunday morning to the smile on her face every time she saw me, my memories of my grandmother will always comfort me.

The memories I recall most fondly are those of Wednesday mornings as a child. I don't remember exactly what we did every week, but I'd go to my grandmother's house and we would spend the morning together. While I suspect she may have told you the time we had together was most impactful on her, I'd have to argue that as a young girl, the time at the local street market, helping her make lunch or listening to her stories, played a key part in who I am today. Not because of what we did or where we went but because I was with a wonderful person who loved me more than I could begin to imagine.

Then there are the memories that will forever take me back and fill me with images, smells, and feelings of my granny. The autumn colours bring a tear to my eye because I know how much she loved the season's beauty. The taste of roasted chestnuts, gratinated butternut squash and just the mention of an apple pie will forever remind me of the love in her kitchen.

I will always have an odd affinity for face cleansers to wash my face in the morning and pink lipstick. And deep down, the perfect night will always be an evening with the family watching football and laughing together.

I've been told more times than I can count that she was incredibly excited for me, the arrival of their first grandchild. But I didn't need to be told this to know it. Whether it be teaching me cooking, pushing me on a swing, pulling me up by each hand for a '1-2-3 Jump!' on walks, or spending countless hours over the years making happy memories with me, I've always known she loved me deeply.

Looking back, it's difficult to see my grandparents as two individuals, as they were always a pair to me. Eventhough my grandfather lived several years longer, being with him at that time always seemed as if my grandmother was just in the other room. Who she was, like any great couple, was part of a whole. Through her actions and wisdom, she taught me how to respect others and how to value things in this world.

Near the end of her life, I made even more beloved memories even though she didn't have the strength to speak or recognize who I was. The once stoic woman I'd grown up with seemed to have lost the exterior shield she'd put up many years before I came into existence.

In addition to all the memories I had, I can now cherish the memory of some of the best hugs she'd ever given me and her huge smiles that showed immense kindness and appreciation.

Even when she wasn't herself anymore, even when she was sleeping all day in a hospital bed without talking, I knew and will forever know she was my granny, and I will always be her "Nocchetta". I will jealously keep her in my memories, like a diamond at the lost and found.

THE GHOSTS ARE ALIVE AND WELL

by Jamie Hafner

Every day, around mid-afternoon, the infamous black double-decker ghost tour bus drives past my building in Newington.

I say infamous because if you live in Edinburgh, you have seen this bus way too often. It lingers on Lothian Road as you attempt to cross, blocks your 29 bus on Princes Street, and is just another nuisance of a tour bus. You cannot escape its presence in this city.

Just a few months ago, this bus would park in front of my building in the Grassmarket every evening. I was frequently greeted by loud, American tourists as they boarded the cheekily decorated bus for a haunted jaunt through Edinburgh.

I moved to Edinburgh's Newington neighbourhood in April. Nowadays, I pass the ghost tour bus fuelling up at the BP petrol station on Ratcliffe Terrace. The elusive, eerie double-decker becomes just another vehicle in a sea of cars waiting to fuel up at the BP.

The bus driver fills the tank with petrol, pays, and drives past my flat every day, towards the place where he once blocked my crosswalk to board tourists. Every night, the ghost bus tour tells visitors of the spirits that roam around Edinburgh.

The guides tell stories about lingering residents of days gone by. Their tours wind around the many cemeteries, chapels, and grey-haired buildings of Old Town. As long as it makes money, every building in Edinburgh has a soul haunting it with a spooky story to tell.

Edinburgh is a haunted city. It is filled with ghosts, but not ghosts that send a shiver down your spine or are worthy of an overpriced ghost tour. These ghosts haunt the residents of the city. They embody the rich spirit of the city.

This spirit is shaped by people that are alive and well. They are your neighbours, co-workers, family, friends. They create the spirit that haunts the entire city.

You think you can sneak away from the ghosts of touristy, crowded Old Town. I thought my everyday life would become much quieter when I moved out of Edinburgh's biggest tourist hub. I thought I would leave behind the screaming, drunk Italians at the overpriced pubs along Grassmarket. I assumed I had said goodbye to the Harry Potter tours cluttering Victoria Street for good. My days of nearly being flattened by for-hire cabs seemed to be over. I thought Edinburgh would finally stop haunting me.

You think you've finally beat them when you make your escape south of the Meadows. The ghosts are everywhere. The ghosts that once lived in Drunk Italians have moved house to the tipsy, talkative twentysomethings taking a drag outside the Meadows Tap. The spirits leading the Harry Potter tours on Victoria Street are now hypnotising the slow walkers on Nicolson. I'm still dodging the phantom-driven for-hire cabs as I walk to the Meadows. And yes, the Edinburgh ghost tour bus can still be seen slipping past my building every day.

The summer weather has forced my windows open in my new Southside flat, letting the spirits in. I hear them in the daily delivery trucks at Sainsbury's, the screaming children after school let out, and the beeping of the walk sign at the crosswalk. The ghosts of the city possess the pub-goers, the slow walkers, and the for-hire cabs in this part of town. The ghosts found new hosts, but they're still the same ghosts.

COOKERY LESSON

by Brian Bourner

Wash hands, check
Flour, check
Eggs, check
Butter, check
Sugar, check
Bicarb, check
Lemon, check
Mix bowl, check
Whisk, check
Oven tin, check
Greaseproof, check
All present and correct
And all the money gone
If I knew you were comin'
I'd've baked a cake,
You said I couldn't
Now watch me make
Easy peasy,
Lemon squeezy,
No problemo
Walk in the park
Cakewalk
Piece of cake
Oven-ready…
Meter money?
Yikes
Slippery soap cake
Bake
Off

FALLING

by Sheila McDougall

Falling in, falling out, falling over

Falling down, falling back, falling foul

Falling behind, falling short, falling under

Falling rain, falling snow, falling ice

Falling leaves, falling hemlines, falling trees

Falling standards, falling markets, falling incomes

Falling interest rates…… fat chance

AN ABLE RACONTEUR

by Gracie Rose

There were stories in his bloodstream,
pounding against his eardrums,
but when he opened his mouth, they'd all tumble out
just words pouring over words
in a jumble - incomprehensible.

They seemed to lose their meaning
the moment he spoke.
The tales in his head
were elegantly woven and meticulously spun,
but they fell apart
when they fell on keen ears.

When no-one else was listening,
he had eloquence even he could not describe.
They would call him articulate, well-spoken -
an able raconteur but
he was none of these things.
His thoughts snagged in his throat
and he choked.

So, he rarely spoke a word at all,
and "a man of few" was dubbed.
He, who had stories in his bloodstream,
beating in his heart,
left them there to gather dust
until they lost all meaning
and became incomprehensible.

AFTER BAGPIPE MUSIC

by Brian Bourner (with apologies to Louis MacNeice)

It's no go the big tick shoes, it's no go the Facebook,
All we want is a life to live and money for some new look.
Their houses are made of old cardboard, their jobs suck more than Dyson
Their flats are lined with pizza boxes and their ears with fashion items.

It's no go the three stripe breeks, it's no go the video walls
It's no go streaming music, and dodgy avatars for pals.
All we want is a quiet pub to plan the revolutions
And some money for hot water to carry out ablutions.

It's no go the Boris liar, it's no go Tory corruption
And police exploiting harmless women.
All we want is a listening ear to hear fear about the weather
All we want is news that's true to stop and have a blether.

Jason Fitzroy went to drink, caught his eye on antiques
Woke to hear vinyl was back, had been revived for weeks.
Grew a beard, but it's still no go his cassette tapes,
All we want is proper art till social media abates.

Populism is fascism, let's call it by its name,
Fosters division and hatred, look away it's war and pain.
It's no go the head in the sand, it's no go the fears
Hope is here it doesn't leave, but always starts with tears.

People are born and people die, the cycle is hardly foreign.
People espy where they go when they die, not where they were before conception.

NO WAY TO DIE

by Sheila McDougall

The machine gun serial numbers
Were 2347 and 7580
No mention of numbers
On the shotguns
Which all but obliterated
The faces of two of the victims
All seven men left lying
In pools of their own blood
Shots were still fired at them
Long after their souls had left this earth
Two of the four gunmen
Dressed as policemen
Adding insult to injury
And hardly reassuring
To the good folk of Chicago
Out buying flowers
For their loved ones
This February 14th

PLAGUE PLAYHOUSE

by Brian Bourner

furl up the flags
unleaf the gold
mute the applause

wrap the stage in mothballs
stay masked
don't wait to be asked

wash and spray
hope to elude
any viruses others exude

show's over
stay home
have hope

don't despair
ride a bike
read a book
eat a pear

FIGHTING FOR WORDS

by Georgina Tibai

INT. FLAT-DAY
A twenty-something girl in her pyjamas sits in front of her computer. Clothes lie all over her unmade bed. A half-drunk cold coffee sits on a pile of handwritten notes on her desk. A smothering of words the screen titled Dissertation. She types with two fingers.

The word uniqiue goes red.
Her eyes narrow.
She deletes the letters up till uniq.
She retypes uniqui, then tentatively finishes it with an e. Uniquie. Red.
She deletes e. Uniqui. Red.
She deletes ui, types uniqie. Red.
Her mouse hovers over the word. A small box offers sweet temptation. Click to view suggestions.
No.
Uniquei. Red.
Her eyes widen. She knows! She deletes the i.
Unique. She is hesitant to press space.
No red. Victory! With a sigh of relief, she leans back on her chair.
Her mouse goes to Review, then Word Count. She clicks.
Word count: 17
She closes the Word Count window and continues with renewed focus.
She writes solition.
It's red.

AFTER THE PARTY
[a short radio play]

by Brian Bourner

Characters
Yvette (Y): Late twenties, smart clothes, carrying a handbag
M (M): Late twenties, smart-casual clothes
J (J): Middle aged, jeans and polo shirt
Bob (B): Late teens, jeans and polo shirt

Scene One
Location - Inside a black taxi – SFX taxi noise
Time – 4pm, Saturday, March 2023 (the new age of austerity)

Y   And the way that guy kept on about his yacht… What was his name?
M   Oh yes, that guy - Guy
Y   Oh yes, Guy – humblebragging about almost drowning himself when he fell overboard off St Lucia after drinking Cristal champagne all day.
M   It wasn't Cristal that Roger was pouring into our glasses back there.
Y   Some sort of fizzy plonk for the plebs I think. I saw Lucinda take a sip and she screwed her face up at him. And the place - I expected at least a decent three course sit-down – just a buffet – and nachos and melted cheese. I ask you, a 'buffet restaurant', and they called it a Swiss raclette or something. It was definitely cheddar. I thought that fondue business went out with the dinosaurs. Slices of cold ham, potato salad, French bread - and that gateaux! I could have made a better meal at home. To be honest, I think Roger and Lucinda are feeling the pinch.
M   I got that impression too – though admittedly they were paying for everything. Guy could have stumped up. I

heard his virtue-signalling, telling you his usual story about how he started out as a brickie's hod carrier and ended up owning the whole nationwide company. It's sort of true. He did work on a building site for a couple of weeks during college vacations. But it was in his uncle's building firm. His uncle never married. No kids. Guy inherited everything. But anyway, it was only a Saturday lunchtime get-together, Roger just wanting to mark his birthday with some old pals.

Y   Saturday night is more appropriate. Shame about Lucinda's working – what did you say – second job driving nightshift taxis? Lunchtime is more like something for kids, a children's birthday party. The only thing missing was candles on that dreadful cake.

M   Maybe they didn't think about it? They haven't got any kids. Kids are such an enormous expense, aren't they? If you were keen we could maybe think about children in a year or two. Roger's NHS salary must be worth a lot less than when I first met him a few years ago. But at least he's managed to get on the housing ladder – huge mortgage – Lucinda's taxi work must help pay for it. He was gobbling food like he hadn't eaten for weeks. What is it Wodehouse says – he was 'getting himself outside of' - whole platefuls of cold ham, pakora, sausage rolls and samosas.

Y   Hardly the haute cuisine you'd led me to expect. What does Lucinda do?

M   She was waitressing for a couple of years after graduating. Hotel receptionist now… I got some hot runny cheese on my best shirt. One for the dry-cleaner's. Even dry-cleaners charge a fortune these days.

Y   At least we can drop the forced smiles now, and we can have a pleasant evening with a glass of decent wine and some chocolates.

M   That's true. We may not be in Guy's league but we aren't

quite counting the pennies yet.
Y   Well, as we agreed when we moved in together last year, you count your pennies and I'll count mine – except of course for the big things, like me having to pay the rent!
M   You're not going to bring that up again are you? We agreed. You're the rent -and your phone contract of course - but I'm everything else – council tax, gas, electricity, water, broadband, tv licence, tv subscriptions – Netflix, Disney+, Sky, Prime, -food, drink, taxis...
Y   No need to rattle on about it Murdo! I sometimes think dividing up our finances this way suits you because whenever we're out with other people you give the appearance that you pay for me, for everything - meals, alcohol, entertainment, - that certainly seemed to be the impression that bitch Sophie had when she joked that if we were a business partnership I must be the sleeping partner.
M   She was talking about herself, her own business Yvy, not us.
Y   She was implying I sleep with you in exchange for financial support. How does that Sophie besom manage to live so well anyway? What does she do?
M   Her dad made money. Spent years buying old flats cheap, doing them up, then selling them at a fat profit. He moved on to letting them out instead of selling them. Then he let Sophie take over. These days I think there are more than a dozen properties she lets out.
Y   Sounds like easy money to me. That man Cameron she's with. Grinning like a hyena. 'Isn't it great how house prices keep shooting up' he says. I just smiled sweetly. I know you said Cammy's parents bought that place for him when he was a student but it doesn't help. I tried talking to him about my work. He said he was sure I made a most wonderful shop assistant – I am not a shop assistant Murdo!

M   Of course you aren't Yvy. You're in retail, you're the deputy manager of a classy little bijou boutique in the St James Quarter, Edinburgh's very own Le Marais.
Y   There's still that prat James ranks above me; thinks he's God's gift. But I could hear that Sophie sniggering behind my back, implying to your friends that I was some kind of kept woman.
M   That's a little paranoid Yvy. You make it sound like she was trying to undermine you, gas lighting you.
Y   She sort of threatened to come into my shop and make me serve her while she tried on our most expensive dresses – talked about haute couture – wouldn't know haute couture if it fell on her head. Well, anyway, gas lighting would be up to you. You certainly wouldn't want to stump up for gas lighting.
M   You're right there. The way fuel and food prices have been rocketing up I think I got the worst of the bargain when we divided up our overhead costs.
Y   The rent's not cheap Murdo. And I think they're planning to put it up again soon.

Scene Two
Location – Front door of flat on their arrival home
Time – 4.30pm, Saturday afternoon

M   *[about to put key in door]*   The fares these black cabs charge is really getting beyond a joke Yvy.
Y   Well I don't understand why you've let the garage keep our car all this time. That must be three weeks now they've been working on it. I mean how much repair work needs doing after an MOT? Unless you make a fuss tradesmen are just in no hurry at all these days are they?
M   I know Ubers and minicabs look a bit cheap to you Yvy, but honestly these days you can make a good case for just taking the bus – a proper and sensible thing to do -

fighting climate change and so on. The bus would have been just as quick....Wait a minute, did you forget to lock the door?
Y   No, of course not. And you were last out as usual.
M   *[peering closely at the lock]*   Well anyway, it's still open. Hells bells Yvy, it looks like the lock's been forced.
Y   Oh God, has someone broken into the flat?
M   There's a light on inside. I can hear people talking. We should call the police.
Y   *[striding into the flat]*   Oh for God's sake Murdo. These days the police won't bother getting here for hours, maybe days. I pay the rent on this place; I pay for that door. I'll bloody well sort this out myself!
J   *[rising from a kneeling position in the hall]*   Oh, ah, hullo there. Just back are you eh? Been on holiday?
Y   Holiday? ... *[aside* how do we divide up the cost of holidays?] ....You've been caught red-handed, give yourself up...
J   Knocked and rang the bell. No answer. Let myself in.
Y   *[threatening to hit Jack with handbag]*   Let yourself in? Who the hell do you think you are breaking into my flat?
J   Ah, hang on, see missus, you've got the wrong end of the stick there...
Y   *[Yvette startled as Bob pokes his head out from the under-the-stairs cupboard]*   Another one! And who the hell is that?
J   Ah, well this little chap would be Bob. We work as a team see, I.....
Y   A bloody gang of thieves. Murdo, there's two of them! Don't let them escape. Block the door. *[She searches in her handbag and pulls out a pair of nail scissors.]* Try to run and I swear I'll poke your eye out with these.
B   Easy on there missus, we're only swapping the meters aren't we.

Y   What do you mean, 'swapping the meters'?

J   Well we're Northern Gas missus. [*Jack turns and points to the writing on the back of his polo shirt – 'Northern – it's a gas, gas, gas'*] Just here to do the meters … gas meter…

B   …and I'm on the electricity…

Y   [*perplexed, brandishing scissors*] 'Do the meters?' 'Do the meters?'

J   Yes, both … your dual fuel contract see…

B   You'll have had all the text messages…

J   …Or emails…

B   …The envelopes with big red lettering.

M   [*slapping his forehead*] Ah, oh dear, my goodness. Well, now I think about it I might be able to explain some of this Yvy.

Y   What do you mean, 'explain'?

M   Well, it's true, there were emails – rather a lot of emails in fact – and then there was a letter… letters… – printed in red.

J   Yes, that's right, see that's how it works missus.

Y   Good God Murdo, are you trying to tell me that these… these people, really are Northern Gas employees, and they've broken into my flat…

J   Well not 'broken in' – that's not right missus. All legitimate, above board. See gas, water, electric – right of entry anytime – case of emergency and so on, so…

Y   …broken into my flat because, because, because they're converting, force-fitting, turning our gas and electricity meters into prepayment meters, because, because…

J   Because the bills haven't been paid, have they missus? Payments stopped weeks ago. Company left with no choice.

Y   [*turning angrily on Murdo*] For God's sake Murdo, is this true? How could you forget to arrange the direct debits? That's all it takes – a little bit of competent household management. No need to stand there looking like you've lost a pound and found a penny. Get it sorted!

M *[shame-faced]*   Ah, well, actually it is a little more complicated than that really. I did set up the direct debits pretty well, but, well…

B Stopped working, did they? - No money in the bank account? – *[aside]* that's usually the way of it, isn't it Jack?

Y *[stunned]*   No money!?... but surely… automatic bank overdraft….

M Yvy you know when I said at least we aren't quite counting the pennies yet, well, actually it's not quite true. To be honest…

Y *[hitting Murdo with her handbag]*   No money?...No money in your bank account?...

M *[squirming, ashen faced]*   Sorry, even the overdraft up to the hilt. Financially embarrassed. Skint. Boracic… See, it's the job.

Y What's wrong with the job? Working hard, going out to the Brewery's offices every day, pottering about filling in computer forms and spreadsheets, - you say it'll all be fully automated soon, but not yet, no not yet, - then home by six-thirty every day. You've always enjoyed admin, clerical work. What's wrong with the job?

M The thing is, when the government pandemic subsidies – furlough and so on – stopped, the beer prices still went up - drinkers cutting back, pubs closing, exports plummeting – bloody Brexit - they just didn't need so many people to organise deliveries…

Y You've lost your bloody job!?

M That's the long short Yvy. Two months ago. Negligible redundancy money - not there long enough. But then your shop re-opened and you were busy checking stock, encouraging sales, helping on the counter, still people with money out there… and I, well I've been, eh, hanging around, walking around the parks mainly, hoping my savings would stretch till I found a new job. Hoped your salary might tide us over if I had to ask. Actually, lots of vacancies out there – hotel cleaners, burger flippers, call centres – that kind of thing - zero hours – how do people live on those wages? I even looked at fast food bicycle delivery...

B Your legs aren't strong enough guv, nothing personal, just saying. Amount of deliveries you got to do to make a living wage... needs strong legs...

M And people cutting back anyway – can't afford delivery – cost of food up nearly 20% - Just Eat, Deliveroo – all letting people go or forcing them to be self-employed again – companies never made a profit anyway, and...

J Driving though? – You could drive a van – help clog up the streets like all those Asda and Amazon and...

M ... and utilities company vans.

J Here, somebody's got to fit PPM. It's a living.

M Maybe not for anyone with scruples? A bit morally dubious sometimes? Cutting off heating – kids – old people - disabled...left freezing, hungry...

Y For God's sake Murdo. You're the bloody slough of despond. At least the rent's paid. Yes me, still paying the rent!

M Oh well that will keep Sophie happy at least – the only way I managed to find a flat...

Y Oh, I see. That's great! Our landlady – that bitch! And the car in the MOT garage – no doubt the repair bill's still unpaid?

M *[apologetic]* And the tax, insurance, not to mention petrol... One thing just seems to lead to another...

Y *[aggressive]* Oh for God's sake, get a grip Murdo. Listen, it can't be too hard to learn how to convert meters can it? – and it looks like there's going to be a lot of demand for people to do these conversions for some time yet…so…do you want to eat or do you want to have scruples?

M   *[brightening up]*   You're not wrong Yvy. It's an idea. In fact you could be absolutely right. I'll get on to Northern Gas right away. [*Turning to the workmen*] What are your names again boys - Jack, Bob is it? – Any chance you could put in a word, give me a decent reference?

Scene Three
Location – Pavement outside shop doorway. It is raining.
SFX rainfall
Time – One month later – 9am Monday
Murdo - unshaven, dirty clothes, sitting cross-legged on pavement, paper coffee cup in front of him alongside a piece of cardboard with 'Hungry and homeless' scrawled on it.
Yvette - striding along the pavement holding an umbrella, suddenly stops, aghast, stands over him, staring down at him.
SFX footsteps coming to sudden halt

Y My God, is that you Murdo?

M Ah, it's you Yvy. Yes, I'm afraid so. You never think it could happen to you, do you? Then you fill in all the stuff to apply for Universal Credit and it takes forever. You fall through the bloody trapdoor before you even realize it's there. Penniless. On the street.

Y You could have been fixing gas meters.

M Couldn't bring myself to do it in the end Yvy. Heart-breaking. There again, they only hire and pay wages to people with a fixed address. Bit of a Catch-22 there, the old 'no fixed abode'. Couldn't even get a job pouring coffee – mentioned body odour, wrong image for customers. You know Yvy, they always said money is the main reason couples argue and break up, but I didn't properly understand… I know you chose the role of paying the rent but, well, I didn't think you'd take it so seriously, react so badly to my new-found, er, impecuniousness… poverty… I had nowhere to go. Are you still living there?

Y I managed to get back in touch with Guy. He spoke to Sophie. She's letting me stay in the flat rent-free for a couple of months until I find some flat-sharers. Couple of people in the boutique are interested – shop takings are down – staff salaries not keeping up with inflation – employees rents still shooting up - lots of people looking for cheaper places to live.

M James, by any chance?

Y Well yes, he has expressed a strong interest. With the rent going up and pay in the boutique not moving Sophie says I'd be better off working for her – property management assistant.

M *[aside, under his breath]* bloody rent collector putting the squeeze on.   Spare some change Yvy? I can barely afford to eat – prices getting ludicrous. Citizens Advice gave me a voucher for the food bank but I'm soaked through, hoping to get enough for a hostel bed tonight.

Y *[dropping some coins into Murdo's cup as she turns away]* Look, I've got to get to work. Money's a bit tight. Cost of food's high for everyone. My present post may not pay too well Murdo but, looking at you, things could be much worse. Maybe I'll see you around.

M Maybe. Goodbye Yvy. Hope James is good for you. *[aside, peering into the paper cup]* No need to despair old son, looks about enough there for a couple of cans – funny, working in a brewery I always fancied wine - but if special brew can blank me out of this for a while… help me forget the state of the world….well, oblivion beckons.

FRIDAY THE THIRTEENTH

by Helen Parker

Hello?
Hi Sis.
Oh, hi Owen. How're you doing?
Fine thanks. How are you?
Exhausted.
That's new! You're usually up with the lark and bouncing.
Spent the night in a broom cupboard.
What?
It was Alexander's prom. End of year jolly. Parents were invited for the first hour, before the teens took over and all hell broke loose.
So this prom was held in a broom cupboard?
Don't be daft. See... I was wearing a yellow dress. Remember that friend of Alex... that high functioning autistic girl... the one that won all the prizes?
Anastasia?
Aye, that's the one. She can't cope with yellow. I had temporarily forgotten, and I didn't want to spoil the poor girl's evening. These occasions are hard enough for her as it is. So when I spotted her I remembered about yellow, so I nipped into the broom cupboard, so she wouldn't see me and get upset. Then the janitor came and locked the cupboard to prevent any kids getting up to any hanky-panky in there.
Didn't you have the presence of mind to bang on the door, or yell?
Owen, have you ever experienced the decibels at these proms?
Why didn't you phone someone?
Putting the phone in my pocket would have spoiled the line of my dress.
But when you didn't arrive home, didn't George raise the alarm?

He was on night shift.
And Alex?
You'd rather not know.
But didn't you say you'd bought something new, specially? A mauve print suit?
Aye, I did. But, you remember that Alex's girlfriend's mum gave us some strawberry jam?
Strawberry jam... ?
Yes. Well, it was in the fridge and we hadn't even opened it. We don't eat much jam. And I thought that if Alex's girlfriend saw it, she might tell her mum, and she'd think we were unappreciative, so I thought I'd better scoff a quick spoonful. And I spilt it. On my mauve print suit. So I had to change.
'Cos you didn't want to offend Alex's girlfriend's mum.
Yes. Because her brother and his wife are neighbour to the Middletons.
Alex's girlfriend's brother and his wife are...
No! Owen, why don't you ever listen! Alex's girlfriend's mum's brother...
Anyway, who are the Middletons?
You know, Kate's parents.
Oh, those Middletons.
YES!
Wait, let me get this straight. You ate a spoonful of strawberry jam because you wanted to stay in the good books of Alex's girlfriend's mum because her brother has antsy neighbours.
Famous neighbours! I didn't say they were antsy! How do you know they're antsy? You've never met them!
But you... oh, never mind. Let's get back to the broom cupboard. How long were you in there?
About twelve hours, I reckon.
But didn't you need the...
Well yes. But the jani keeps his cleaning bucket in there.
Ah, his bucket.
Yes. His bucket.

Hmm.
Yes.
But didn't you feel cold in the broom cupboard all night?
Not too bad. I put on all the overalls hanging on the back of the door, and sat on a rolled up mat that used to be in the head's office.
And you didn't get out until school began the next morning?
No! It's the end of term. No school. When George got home and Alex finally missed me, he phoned round his pals and it was Anastasia who knew where I was.
Anastasia? The girl with the high-functioning...
Yes! She must've spotted me. She and Alex arranged to meet at school and they had to get the jani and show him where I was.
So he unlocked the door and you gave Anastasia a tizzy because of your yellow dress?
No. 'Cos by then, the front was white.
Er...
It was dark in the broom cupboard. I hadn't taken my phone so I didn't have a torch. Had to find my way around by feel. But it all smelt nice and clean. There was a high shelf. Someone hadn't screwed the top on the bleach bottle properly, so when I pulled it down, it spilled all over the front of my dress.
Bleach.
Aye. It takes the colour out of...
I know what bleach does.
But, as I said, there were overalls hanging on the back of the door, so while the dress was drying, I wore those.
So when the jani opened the door, with Alex and Anastasia by his side, there you were in a yellow dress with a white skirt, squinting in the bright light, after spending the night in a broom cupboard because you spilt jam on your other suit because you didn't want to offend the relatives of the future king.

Well done Owen. Finally. It's not like you to be so slow off the mark.

This must surely be the worst case I've ever heard of Friday the thirteenth bad luck.

Don't be daft! I'm not superstitious. Anyway, this all happened on Thursday. Today is Friday. Today was lucky Friday cos I was rescued. Just because you moved to New Zealand and get everything before us - Christmas Day, New Year's Day, your birthday, Friday the thirteenth, you forget that the rest of us are twelve hours behind. But that reminds me...

What?

I ought to warn the janitor about the bucket. Otherwise, he'll think Friday the thirteenth has brought him bad luck and he'll become superstitious...

THE COST OF LIVING

by Annie Foy

Difficult? She was unbearable. Unlovable as a wife and as a mother. Two sons, one escaped to Australia, one to the Merchant Navy. I'm sure my father's early death was his escape. And I, spinster daughter: we may not use such terms any more, but we certainly understand the concept. Undereducated, obedient and required to stay at home as domestic help, then nurse for Father, then carer for the increasingly frail and crabbit old witch.

But she had a hard life, she was a refugee, an orphan... Oh, shut up! I know it, she told me every day. None of it excused her character. Every damned day I was made to sit and listen and look as she pored over her aged maps and dragged her bony finger from east to west, over countries that haven't existed since before Victoria reigned. Here lived her aristocratic ancestors, pushed this way and that by empires and rebels, Ottomans and Prussians. Here her family were driven, and here, and here. And finally her small gaggle of peasant aunts and uncles, with their handcarts and headscarves found their way here. Left unpersecuted, they all lived long lives, and she was the last of those survivors. Keeper of ancestral memories and starched lace doilies. Keeper of several small inheritances, to be shared with no one, certainly not me. I had Carer's Allowance and free board, what more did I want?

I wanted to be rid of her without any cost to myself, financial or otherwise.

The central heating system was ancient and risked becoming dangerous or failing permanently. But no, of course not. She would not hear of replacing it, would not be tricked into parting with her money, even though a generous grant was available. It was a scam. The Socialists would not steal this house. The Bolsheviks would not win this time.

Then there was some publicity about the requirement to have smoke and carbon monoxide detectors installed in every home. I learned about leaking gas boilers and about the signs and symptoms of carbon monoxide poisoning. Hmm. Apart from the bright red skin discolouration, those symptoms might all have other, non-sinister causes. *Google Images* showed that this would be substantially more than a rosy glow. Would a loving daughter fail to notice that? And what kind of devil wouldn't succumb at the same time?

I told her that I had to have a short break, there was no point in arguing or threatening. I had booked a three-night stay in a comfortable guest house by the sea. She could just get on with it. I stocked the refrigerator with her favourite home-made dishes: beetroot and turnip treats, liberally salted. Everyone would see what a caring daughter I was. I slipped a note through a neighbour's letterbox telling them I would be away, but forgetting to write my phone number in case of emergency. Oops.

My step was light as I took a cup of tea to her bedside and carried my weekend bag downstairs. After washing up my breakfast things, I took a few hundred pounds from her secret cache, switched on the central heating and blew out the pilot light. I locked the door behind me.

How awful to return from my first holiday in three years to find my dear mother dead, in bed where I had left her.

What luck that I had invested in a substantial insurance policy on her life. How wonderful to now have a very high quality central heating system, installed as part of the complete refurbishment of my home. Other improvements include an Open University degree course, a substantial upgrade to my wardrobe and hair. And three tattoos: a tiger, a wolf and a dragon.

ROSES ARE RED DILLY DILLY

by Helen Parker

'It's no good, Meg! What did I tell you? It just won't work. I can't do it.' George was raising his voice. He hadn't meant to, and glanced behind him guiltily, though he knew no one was there. 'It's just impossible. I told you so.' His voice was quieter now, just a croak.

There was no reply. Had he expected one? After thirty years of marriage, Meg had learned when to speak and when to let him rant. When his anger was spent, she would murmur, 'It's alright, pet. Don't you worry.' She'd pat his hand, and her smile was so engaging, it made George smile, in spite of himself.

'What are *you* looking at?'

Now George directed his irritability at the cat instead of at Meg. It had always been Meg's cat, really, and it despised George. The feeling was mutual. 'If you don't like what you hear and see, why do you keep following me around?'

'Miaou.' It regarded him venomously.

Glancing at his watch, George contemplated missing work. What good was quality control in a factory where machines were made by robots, anyway? But he'd had his quota of time off and after all, he needed something to do. And an income.

He looked at his watch again. Time to make a start, but it was hard to tear himself away. 'I'll have to be going. Traffic's so slow now that South Bridge is closed northbound and there's only buses and trams allowed in Princes Street. I bet the damn car won't start, same as yesterday. It can't stand this cold weather. Like me. And it's not even light yet. I get to work in the dark and I leave in the dark. Might as well be at the North Pole.' He stared in front of him and scowled.

'Here, I brought you these.' Grudgingly, he laid down a dozen red roses. 'Well, it's your birthday. What else could I do?'

His phone buzzed in his pocket. He snatched it and peered at the screen. Cathy.

'Hey, Dad! Guess what? I got the job! I start next month!'

George cleared his throat. 'Ah. Well done lass. Knew you could do it.'

'And Dad? I know it's Mum's birthday. Didn't know if you'd got anything planned. Why don't you meet me and Craig at the Pizza Palace tonight. My treat, to celebrate my job. Didn't want you to be on your own today. New start, Dad.'

'Well, that's thoughtful of you, pet, but I'm…'

'Great! I'll book a table. 7.30, OK? See you then. Bye.'

The girl was right, as usual. Just like her mother. It wasn't exactly that they liked to have the last word; it was more an indefinable ability to assume his agreement. Oh well. It hadn't done him any harm up to now. George bent to reposition the roses, then resolutely turned away and headed out of the cemetery to get the car started and begin the daily round.

50 WORDS A DAY FOR 7 DAYS

by Rebecca 'Bex' Stevenson

Monday
Hey gorgeous lady. How r u? Would love to see your beautiful face again. Brunch yest was ace. Usually don't trust my friends to set up a blind date – I've seen some dogs, haha – but ur a winner. Want to go for dinner and a flick sometime? Luv, Cx

Tuesday
Hi C, Yes, brunch was good - the eggs benedict was amazing. Honestly though, I didn't feel we had loads in common. I know Simon seemed to think we'd get on, but... I don't know... I don't want to mess you about. Maybe we call it quits? Best, E

Wednesday
Ah. My bad. Not sure how I so misread that. #awkward. C

Was it the story about the time I got duct-taped to a lamppost?

Hi C, It wasn't the lamppost story (actually very funny). Sounds harsh, but you were obnoxious, insincere and... "I've seen some dogs". Really? E

Thursday
Hey E, Pls can we start over?? I'd heard good things about you from Si. Then you arrived and were really attractive.... I wanted you to think I was smooth and funny so obvs I behaved like a total wazzock. R u free tomorrow? Saturday? Cx

Also, soz. Cx

Friday
Hi C, Simon just dropped by with an intriguing invitation. On paper? Retro... Ex

Haha, didn't want to freak u out by pitching up at ur house #stalker. Plans for Sat are sorted. U said u like getting dirty? Wear something warm & washable! I've got food covered. Cx

Saturday
Hey C, Got home and into the bath fully clothed. So much mud! Quad-biking was inspired. Who picnics in February, though? How's your tailbone? Sorry I laughed but you looked so alarmed as you slid down the hill! Two hours of high-octane activity, and you injured yourself walking? Ex

Sunday
Morning you. Thanks for yesterday. I had a blast but... OMG my quads this morning! I can barely walk! If you are free later, I know this place just around the corner that does great eggs benedict? Last time I was there I met a really lovely guy... Ex

GOLD

by Helen Parker

Something's afoot, I'm sure of it.

Ever since young Breanna came for her university interview, and I showed her around Edinburgh, there's been something in the air.

'Aunty Mary,' she said, 'I thought Scottish post boxes were red!'

Well, I thought the girl must be stupid until I remembered that Irish ones are green, and she lives in Dublin. But she'd been looking at the gold post box in Hunter Square, dedicated to Sir Chris Hoy. He's always been my Rob's hero. He's even got the same birthday as Rob – March 23rd – though twenty-five years later, of course.

Breanna had said, 'I never knew Uncle Rob before he used a wheelchair.'

More's the pity, I thought. My sister Fiona moved to Dublin all those years ago, and Breanna's her youngest. She'd told Breanna that Rob had been in the cycling squad for the British Commonwealth Games when it was in Edinburgh - in 1970, that was, before Rob's accident. I bet Breanna couldn't even imagine him then. Now all she sees is an old man with disabilities.

But Rob is the one who really deserves a gold medal. He's worked for so long with disabled kids. He's done sponsored activities for all sorts of charities. He's even abseiled off the Forth Bridge in his wheelchair.

Abseiled! That's a misnomer. Hung, more like. He's really brave. But after all he's been through, he said that was nothing!

He's spent years supporting disabled athletes. He's sat on the finishing line, cheering on runners with prosthetic legs. He's coached disabled skiers in the Cairngorms. He's taught swimming to kids with cerebral palsy who were scared stiff of the water, until they saw him being hoisted into the pool and laughing about it. He's talked suicidal kids out of depression and supported them and their parents for years.

He really deserves a gold medal.

Instead, we've got a golden wedding celebration coming up.

But he's struggling now. The years and the pain have finally caught up with him, though he'd never admit it. He never complains, and he still follows his various protégés on Facebook and Twitter.

He follows Sir Chris, as well. What a cyclist! 'He's our champion,' I told Breanna. 'An Edinburgh boy. Six gold medals and one silver. Beijing and London.'

'What about Rio?' the girl had asked.

'No, he's forty-two now. He's moved on to motor racing. Wheels and speed are in his blood.' She laughed when I told her he'd been inspired by the cyclists in *E.T.!*

'Me too!' she'd said. 'I loved that film.'

'Sir Chris started on a BMX. He won races before he was even in his teens. Then he moved on to track events. He married the lovely Sarra – Lady Hoy – in 2010 and they had a wee boy, Callum. Arrived eleven weeks early, he did, and took everyone by surprise. But he's doing well, and now he's got a wee sister, too.'

'Mum told me that Uncle Rob went to Sir Chris's wedding.'

'Ha! That was wishful thinking! No, what happened was – they say Sir Chris tried to keep it quiet, but you know how it is – with a name and reputation like his – everyone wanted to be there to wish him well. So Rob and I hung around outside with hundreds of others, mostly journalists I reckon, to greet him and Sarra when they left the church.'

'Where were they married?'

'St Giles! None but the best for our Chris! Anyway, they came out of the church and took a kind of circuit of the statue and waved and said hello to everyone, before they went into the parliament buildings for their reception. He was in his kilt, of course, and Sarra looked gorgeous.'

I found myself thinking about our own wedding. Rob had worn his kilt, too. Fifty years ago! Can you believe it? It doesn't do to think about the past too much, or what might've been, if Rob hadn't had his accident.

As I said, I suspect Fiona and her brood are planning something. I hope it's not a surprise party. I don't think Rob would be up to it, and I certainly wouldn't enjoy it. We don't need anything gold, either. I've got my ring, and Rob's got his. That's enough.

*   *   *

Young Breanna got into Edinburgh University. She's staying at Pollock Halls now, and she loves her course. And Edinburgh. We get to see her most weeks. That's a treat for us, especially since we were never able to have a family of our own. She's coming round later to take us out for afternoon tea at the Balmoral. Her mum's paying – it's an anniversary treat, she says. Rob and I have spruced ourselves up. We're quite the dashing couple, even if I say so myself.

Here's the postman. 'Rob! There are some cards for us!' I take the cards into the sitting room where he's reading the paper.

'My word! Look at all these!' he says. 'How kind of people to remember.' I'm smiling at him, because he's the kind one, the one who thinks of other people. Lots of the cards are from his past pupils, or families he's supported over the years. But here's a very special one. It's big and gold and Rob's opening it carefully. He's staring at it and he's gone quite pale.

'What is it pet?'

'Come and look.'

I'm reading the beautiful card over his shoulder.
To Rob and Mary, a gold medal couple, with kindest regards from Chris and Sarra Hoy.

SLIPPING OUT THE FRINGE

by Brian Bourner

'Ok, Ah'll kick aff wi "Whit's the maist popular colour in a boozer?... It's maroon!" '

'Oh aye, "Ma roon.". No bad. Braw. But it'll no dae son. Yer oan a slippery slope wi that yin amang Hibbies frae Leith.

'Right, ok. Ah could stairt wi' ancient stuff tae get the punters in the mood – lik whit's the difference atween Bing Crosby an Walt Disney?'

'Bing sings an Walt disnae. Son, this is the Fringe. New material. No stuff deid an buried in the vaults lang syne.

'Weel whit aboot the tourist wumman, loups oan the bus an asks fur a Noddy ticket? Driver disnae ken whit she's oan aboot. She says she's gonnae jouk aboot the toon, oan an aff buses, gaun different places, an a Noddy ticket wis whit she wis telt tae ask fur. Bus no movin. Back o the bus punter bawls "Gie the wumman 'an aw day' ticket an get a bend on afore she's gien a parkin ticket anaw."

'Naw, Noddy an Big Ears are nae use. Bairns' characters niver go doon weel. No a road tae go doon. Slippery slope son.'

'Ach awright, weel whit aboot a riddle? 'Whit wey does a stane fly up in the cloods?... It's a laverock?'

'Oh aye, a rock. Naw, that'll no dae neither. Dinnae be a numptie. Even hauf the posh punters frae Laverockbank willnae ken whit a laverock is. Jist dinnae start in wi thae wurds awright, jist gonnae no.'

'How no though? Got a guid yin aboot an auld wifie an a bubblyjock. The auld besom's new in the country an lookin oot fur the company o a young chiel. Asks a pal tae find her a lively Scotsman, 'a bubbly Jock', an…'

'Aye, aye, gets lumbered wi a turkey. Ah've telt ye. Nane o that.'

'This is hoo it stairts though is it no eh? Thin end o the wedge. D'ye want us tae end up lik Francis Jeffrey?'

'Frankie? Who he? Whit ye spraffin oan aboot?'

'Mind, yon chiel that scuttled awa tae Lunnon an come back tae Edit the Embra Review? Judge Braxfield spiered "That laddie has clean tint his Scotch and found nae English". It's a gey slippery slope tae skite aboot oan auld yin. Ye think yer jist gien folk a haun tae unnerstan yer accent, an afore ye ken whaur ye are yer in a richt fankle, ye've forgot hoo tae spier yer ain Scots leid, yer ain tongue.'

'Ach, ya wee nyaff, yer haiverin.'

'Naw Ah'm no… Ach, awa an bile yer heid. Ah've hid ma lot, Ah'm offski.'

'Yer cruisin fur a bruisin mair like. It's the morn's morn yer oan son an it's ower late tae get a haud o a sub afore yon time. Some scunner thon wid be. Ah'm tellin ye, yer daein it, like it or no, or Ah'll gie ye yer heid tae play wi.'

'Ach, gie's peace auld yin, yer wearin oot ma lugs wi yer bletherin an Ah'm wabbit. The gemme's a bogey. An onywey, yer howff's mockit, totally mingin, Ah'm gien it a body swerve. Ah need mair'n a day tae scrieve new stuff. Ah'm gonnae redd-up an awa. Ye'll jist hae tae gie yer auld money tree a shake an see if some ither daft galoot o a comic faws oot.'

THE DAY THE COLOURS CAME TOGETHER

by Sylvia Simpson

Red was a happy apple in a crowd of friends who admired his fiery hue and desired to be loving and happy like him. But Red didn't always feel good. He often felt lonely even though he had lots of friends. "Maybe Orange will help me feel better," said Red.

"How joyful it is to see you," Orange enthusiastically replied, jumping energetically and taking Red in her arms. "You always know how to help me feel better," sniffed Red. "Sometimes a warm embrace is all you need," Orange murmured snuggling into Red's arms. A smile crept up on Red's face.

Yellow the banana sang, "We are better together, together, together." Simultaneously, Red and Orange quizzically asked Yellow what his words meant. "Oh, wonderful pals," replied Yellow. "We need each other. Without colour there is no brightness, no difference and no 'WOW'. Everything would be sadly boring." Let's find more friends.

"Oh, just look at me. My skin is hard and bumpy," cried Green the avocado. "Why do I have to be the odd one?" Just then Red, Orange and Yellow stumbled onto Green who took the chance to snuggle up to them, forgetting her negative feelings. "Let's help someone else…"

Blue the blueberry had a problem. He didn't know if he was too small or too big. "I'm a teeny blueberry, but when I paint the sky blue it's too vast and the clouds get in the way." To the rescue came Red, Orange, Yellow and Green, "Come, come friend…"

Indigo, the plum was shy, secretive, almost never saying a word. His eyes would scan everyone and his lips kept tightly shut. This made it hard for Indigo to have friends.

Luckily Red, Orange, Yellow, Green and Blue, all snuggled together, loved making friends and making them feel included and loved.

Violet the aubergine was wise, creative and imaginative. She would sit, or stand, or jump, or run whilst her imagination raced with stories of the fine day when Red, Orange, Yellow, Green, Blue, Indigo and herself came and worked together to create the most brilliant RAINBOW!

"Better together'" they sang.

FOR RICHER, FOR POORER

by Helen Parker

'This new boyfriend, Robert...'

'Robin!'

'Ah, Robin. He's in finance, you say?'

'Sort of.'

'Doesn't look like a banker, with his green hoodie and tight trousers.' The aristocratic maternal nose wrinkled. 'And he comes from the north-east of the city? Woodthorpe, maybe? Such a nice area...'

'Sherwood.'

'Ah, Sherwood. Does he have an office in the Old Market Square? I do hope he has good prospects. Not like those other...'

'*Don't*, Mother! Don't criticise everything. My boyfriend, our clothes, my friends...'

'*Such* friends, Marian. How could you...' Needles of ice. 'That big oaf, John Little, William Red-something, the Reverend Puck...

'*'Tuck!'*

'Anyway, who heard of a friar cooking? Only women cook...'

Anger choked Marian. 'If you disapprove of everything, why did you...?'

She already knew, but her mother answered, 'We adopted you because we felt it our duty to share our wealth with someone less fortunate, dear. Surely we are entitled to some respect and appreciation...'

In bed fully clothed, Marian waited for his owl hoot, climbed out, met him on tiptoe.

'Found it, babe. The perfect squat. Our home.' She hugged him, and followed silently down tree-lined avenues. 'This way, through the yard. Everyone's here.'

Hearts of oak, generous spirits, lovers of justice.

'Food's hot. Tuck in.'

'Beef burgers?' Marian asked.

'Venison. Compliments of the County Sheriff!'

A shared meal, merry company and a cool, green, relaxing ambiance.

'*Now* I'm rich!' she said. 'I love you, Robin.'

THE DANGER OF DOPPELGANGERS

by Jamie Hafner

I saw my old 4-H Club leader, Deb, at a bakeshop this morning. She was nibbling on a scone as she caught up with a friend over tea. Her once auburn locks were now long and grey after rounds of chemotherapy. The loss of her son in 2018 aged her quickly. She had lost the spark in her eyes and the glow in her skin, but she was still the woman who taught me how to bake so many years ago. Her friend was in the middle of a riveting story about her sister. Their conversation made Deb chuckle. As she laughed, a smile burst from her lips.

Seeing her in an Edinburgh Bakehouse was odd, as she resides in a stately stone farmhouse just a few miles outside my American hometown. The home sits just beyond the main road, nestled between cattle barns and chicken coops. I loved hearing the cows coo on Saturday mornings before our club meetings. They greeted us on foggy winter mornings as our club members trudged up her driveway, recipe books and sewing machines in tow.

Seeing her across the cafe dining room was equally bewildering as she died two years ago of breast cancer.

The same encounter occurred just yesterday aboard the 31 bus to Bonnyrigg. As I settled into my seat, I felt the gentle tap of another foot on mine. I looked up and saw an old woman, embarrassed by her foot misplacement. I flashed a forgiving smile her way, only to realize that she bore an uncanny resemblance to my primary school librarian. Draped across her stocking-encased legs was a navy blue skirt that matched her deep blue loafers. She had a rolling shopping bag half full of goods from Edinburgh's fading high street shops. Her ensemble mirrored my old librarian's signature style, and her face bore the same familiar contours.

Though I forget her name, I remember her wrinkled face, her button nose, and her kind eyes. Her soothing whisper filled my younger self with such calm every time I checked out a library book. She always made sure I grabbed a freshly stamped bookmark on my way out the door. My primary school librarian also passed a few years back of a disease which I have chosen to forget.

I've been able to see dead people for a few years now. Not in the Long Island Medium way though, but in the most unfortunate way: I see them in doppelgangers. Those pesky lookalikes frequently wander across my path, reminding me of the heartache I packed away years ago.

For the life of me, I have never been able to find a living friend's doppelganger. Yet, when I least expect it, I am bombarded by copies of people who are long gone. This week, it was my school librarian and my 4-H leader; next week it will be an old classmate who was killed in a car accident or a church member that's been six feet under for over a decade. I've learned that the only thing worse than being haunted by the dead is being haunted by the living.

For when the ghosts take human form, they gain stronger leverage over you. Doppelgangers of the Dead give you a taste of the past. For a moment, you are tricked into thinking that they are still here, right in front of you, ready to reunite. Only when you look deep into their eyes do you see who they really are: strangers. You look away to avoid an awkward encounter, but it is too late to avoid the pain of the doppelganger's presence. The damage is done.

I can't be certain if these strangers actually look like the people from my past. My mind may be playing a cruel trick on me, placing faces on strangers who are just understudies for the real deal. Whether it is real or just pretend, I'll never know.

All I know is that I saw my old 4-H club leader across the cafe dining room this morning, enjoying her life again

after all the pain and heartache from cancer, from burying a child.
    For a moment I was happy for her. All I ever wanted was to see her smile again, and I did.

THE IMPERFECT THINGS

by Stéphanie Voytier

BANG! The sound was dull, definite. She didn't need to turn around, she knew what had fallen. A vase. THE vase, the one she'd made at the pottery class a week before. Everyone had marvelled at her creation. Even the teacher, so stern, so melancholic, had cracked a smile when she saw it. Her provision bag must have hit it when she entered the kitchen. Disappointment was now rushing in her, like a river grown wild after a thunderstorm. She turned to face the disaster and sighed. The vase was split in two. A puddle of water was expanding slowly on the tiled floor and the bouquet of dried flowers was soaked. It looked miserable. She picked it up and threw it in the bin. She placed the vase - or rather what was left of it - on the kitchen table and mopped the floor. Then she sat and took the two pieces of clay in her hands. She pressed them firmly together. The crack was almost invisible. Almost. Chips of ceramic were missing here and there but it was doable, she could glue it back to its former shape. Nevertheless, the vase would never be as perfect and nice as it was.

Some people say that imperfect things are the most beautiful things. 'These things tell a story,' they say. 'like people, who are more loveable because of their vulnerabilities and imperfections'. Well, it wouldn't do with this vase. She had liked it perfect. Then a word popped in her mind. Kintsugi. She was surprised to remember it. She'd heard it for the first time a month before when a friend talked about the Japanese art of mending broken objects, with golden lacquer, to enhance rather than hide the cracks. It was supposed to add a 'je ne sais quoi'. She shrugged and said out loud, 'After all, why not? Whatever I do, it won't look as good as before anyway.' She picked up her handbag hanging on the back of a chair and left.

Two hours later, she was back, sitting at the table again, a fine brush in one hand and a piece of the vase in the other. Slowly, she began to stroke the edges of the clay with the tip of the brush glistening with golden lacquer. Very slowly. And she realised that it was like tending the wound of a child. It took gentleness, it required a soft touch, and only TLC could do the job well. Bit by bit she immersed herself in her task and began to relax. For a few precious minutes, she forgot about the mortgage, her daughter's problems at school, her distancing husband, and happy memories of her childhood slowly began to surface, like joyful bubbles in a glass of champagne. The laughter of her dad, the tree-hut in the oak tree, the tenderness in her mother's eyes. It was unexpected, welcome, and she was reluctant to put the brush down when she finished her task. She suddenly said, 'Thank-you!' and felt silly. She even looked over her shoulder to make sure nobody had heard her. No one says thank you to an object. But she knew that the vase, or whatever force or magic had created this moment, had given her a gift. The gift of a momentary escape from the mundane and a brief connexion with her inner child. She had forgotten her. So she was still here... Was she as funny, joyful and careless as before? Could she reach her again?

She pressed the two pieces of the vase together a few minutes to give time to the lacquer to start to glue them. Then she put the vase on the table and smiled. 'Yes, I get it now!' she thought, 'Imperfect things do tell a story.'

ANNA PROCEMO

by John Tucker

The unremarkable building was adjacent to the Parliament. It was a two-storey block which contained two flats as well as a number of offices. These were designed to be convertible into classrooms at a moment's notice. The building was occupied by a staff of translators and interpreters who could be called on whenever the government required translations of foreign correspondence or interpreters for foreign visitors.

The official in charge was the Minister of Security, Sir George Huntington, who had the highest level of security clearance. His secretaries were his daughter Margaret and her husband James, who was also an expert in linguistics.

Margaret and James lived in the flat above the building's entrance. It was next door to the flat used by any visitors that the government had decided ought to be concealed from public view.

From his office at the front of the building James could see anyone entering the building and, on the other side, the canteen area that was visited by the daily police patrol that constantly encircled Parliament on foot. They were friendly with James and when they were off-duty would sometimes drop in to see him before accessing the canteen and mingling with the staff there. They were always in uniform, carrying weapons.

The building had been left as a legacy to Parliament with the proviso that once a year they would take in a rough sleeper, clean them up there, and if necessary teach them to read and write and help them find them a job. It was a peculiar rent to pay.

One day James looked out his window and saw the police bringing a down-and-out to the building. He went downstairs to meet them. They said they had brought a woman for them to look after, mainly because they could not understand the language she spoke. But James was a little suspicious when the police insisted, saying she might run away, that this homeless person should be kept behind closed doors as far as possible while she was with them. The poor girl was giving off a terrible smell, unbelievably dishevelled, her hair dirty and unkempt. In fact her face was so dirty it was impossible to tell her original skin colour. The police reported that she had been found in a shipping container and that they could not make any sense of her babbling.

"So," said the police, "we brought her to you."

"Thanks," James replied sarcastically. However, Margaret took pity on the girl and led her to the empty flat. She pointed to the bath, the linen cupboard, the washing machine, and soaps. Speaking slowly, and using gestures she hoped might help her understand, Margaret added "If you need anything, just give me a call."

Returning to her own flat Margaret spoke to James. "Strange clothes our new visitor is wearing. Skirt and waistcoat all made of very fine, light tan coloured leather. Good quality high heeled boots too, as well as long leather gloves and a hooded cape. Everything's well-tailored in the same material. It will take some cleaning!"

Later on that day Margaret knocked on the door of the flat where she had settled the visitor and entered to find an elegantly dressed and beautifully pristine young woman with light blue eyes. She was tall, with a mass of black hair and an ivory white smile. Everything was cleaned and in place.

Margaret led her towards the computer, saying "Come with me to the computer and we'll find out what language you speak." James joined them, and after playing with some vowel sounds concluded it was a dialect of a Peruvian language.

Only then did the visitor speak. "My name is Anna Procemo. I also speak English."

Margaret was so taken aback that all she could think to say was "Let's eat. James is a very good cook."

As they sat down to dinner Anna did not speak much but asked three questions.

Speaking aside to Margaret, James whispered "Three questions from Anna in quick succession. Maybe she's a journalist? When I ask her a question she never gives a straight answer. She's evasive, like a politician."

Addressing Anna, Margaret asked. "Would you like to help with clearing the dishes?"

"No "said Anna, with a sudden definiteness."Anna does not carry! Margaret will switch on the computer again for me please."

The following day, James said to Margaret, "If she won't help with the washing up see if she will push the barrow round with today's mail and meet the staff."

Most of the language experts were young women around Anna's age. They fussed around her in a friendly way, understanding of her current circumstances as a rescued rough sleeper. They were full of admiration for the fashion of her clothing, and Margaret murmured to one of the translators. "She won't take anything off, not the hood, the cloak, the waistcoat, those high heeled boots, not even her gloves."

But the language experts were keen to get closer to Anna. One of them suggested "Come and be part of our competitive line dancing group, your boots will fit in well with our cowboy clothes. We badly need another member to be able to enter a full team. If you join us it will please James because otherwise he'll be press-ganged into making up the numbers.

The next evening Anna was smiling with her ivory white teeth, obviously greatly enjoying line dancing with the ladies as they practised in the lecture room behind the canteen.

The day after that James said to Margaret "Maybe you could take her shopping and let her push the trolley. And when you have all the fresh vegetables we need you could proceed to find out how our last rescued protégé, Aly, is settling in with the Professor in the museum."

On their arrival in the museum Aly appeared. He was delighted to see Margaret and suggested "Come and see the Prof's latest acquisition. He's trying to decipher this old carved stone from South America. No-one seems to have the ability to read the writing. After introductions and getting a good report from the Professor of Aly's settling into work Anna stepped forward towards the ancient stone and straight away read what was written there.

"King Akiteea sorely oppressed his people so that one day a shaman came and led away all of his people. The children of the mountain mist travelled into the forest and were never seen again. The King died alone in an empty kingdom."

"That's amazing!" exclaimed to Professor. "It's a morality tale! I hope you're not having me on."

Margaret only smiled and said "We've got to go, Anna has line dancing practice tonight."

Anna loved the stomping line dancing, practising with the women in her square heeled boots. It brought a smile to her face, showing her ivory teeth. She blended in well with the fancy dress bunch and appreciated the country music.

Unfortunately, the following day Margaret ended up in hospital with serious facial cuts after being caught up in a multiple car crash. When James and Anna arrived at her bedside the nurse said "There are so many casualties we badly need Margaret's bed."

But Anna said to the nurse "Can you come back in a minute?" Then, when the nurse had left the room, Anna took off her gloves to reveal long orange coloured fingers. She took hold of Margaret's head with them and, lo and behold, when she took her fingers away the facial cuts had healed. The scars were disappearing and then were gone. "Now let's go" said Anna.

James was dumfounded but just glad to get Margaret home. Fearing no-one would believe him he only spoke of the event later with Sir George.

During the next evening, while line dancing practice was taking place, the hall doors burst open and three large men strode in holding guns, one pointing his revolver at Anna.

"You!" he yelled, in a foreign accent. "Come with us or I'll shoot. Believe me I have diplomatic immunity and won't be arrested for your murder."

Then a new voice was heard. The regular police patrol had been visiting the canteen and had looked in to watch the line dancing women from a corner at the back of the hall. "Drop your weapons!" they ordered. "Our bullets don't recognise diplomatic immunity."

There was a clang as revolvers hit the floor. The threat of a major diplomatic incident, together with a lot of swear words in an unknown tongue, saw the intruders leave the building.

On hearing the commotion Sir George had appeared. He said to James "I'll make some phone calls. In the meantime take Anna to Northolt RAF station and ask for a captain Hetherington. He'll fly you both to Paris where a diplomat will give you short term visas and papers allowing you both to fly to Lima. Anna will be met there. Come straight back alone afterwards. Don't ask. I'll tell you all about it when you return. Now go quickly."

After arriving in Lima and getting through passport control Anna and James stepped out onto the airport balcony and saw a reception committee of six shamen waiting for her below. They were dressed in feather head-dresses. They had painted bodies, bare feet, gold armbands, and short feathered batons. They were moving to the rhythm of flutes and drums. On spotting Anna they leapt in the air and fell to their knees, stretching their arms to the ground before them in a gesture of worship.

Anna stood tall, firstly raising her arms upward in a Y shape, then pointing her open palms and long orange fingers upward. She then lowered her arms, folded them across her bosom, and bowed, at which point a mighty roar erupted from a now rapidly gathering crowd, and the music grew louder and louder.

Anna turned to her companion and said "Thank you James. Now you can go home and look after Margaret and the baby." James frowned, bewildered at this mention of a baby, but Anna was already parading away with her followers, heading in the direction of the forest.

Margaret and Sir George were waiting when he arrived home. The first thing that Margaret said to him was "I've got a surprise for you James!"

To which James replied "There's a baby coming."

"How, how on earth did you know?" stammered Margaret, flabbergasted.

"Anna told me." James turned to Sir George. "Who was she really?"

Sir George replied "Anna is a shaman. She has the power and influence to control all of Peru. It was no wonder some people were looking for her to prevent her return to that country. They wanted to control her."

James smiled ruefully at Margaret. "You know," he said, "there are some things in this world that mere mortal men will never understand."

TESCO IN WINTER

by Sheila McDougall

Bright lights
Fake greenery
Mince pies
2 for 1
3 for 2
A dazzling array
But not for the likes
Of Shuftie McTuftie
Who hangs around
Outside in the cold
Looking for lost change
Items left in trolleys
Discarded sandwiches
Anything to comfort and warm

ANOTHER GROUNDHOG DAY IN LOCKDOWN

by Brian Bourner

Another groundhog day in lockdown
fast as a glacier, exciting as bog
I guess again I'll stay at home again
where the jigsaw is progressing
like algae over a stagnant loch
like moss stealing over my phone.

Another groundhog day of lockdown
of hermits living in a fog
I guess I'll grin and bear it
the peace and quiet and no job.

Another groundhog day of lockdown,
more weather to contemplate.
Shadows apart for an hour in the sun,
volunteers testing their prison yard.
A nod here and there for pleasantry
across empty silences of roads.
Avoiding media's empty soundbites
from politicians acting dumb.

Another groundhog day of lockdown
of home into substandard office
of bread and circuses just bread
of minimum wagers at foodbanks
of stadia empty enough to shock Juvenal
of sports fans transformed into living dead.

Another groundhog day of lockdown
no culture, cafes, clubs or pubs.
TV and radio on endless repeat,

or DIY and computer games.
And dreams of nearest and dearest
through ghostly video calls to meet.

Another groundhog day of lockdown
empathy growing for Jeffrey Lewis,
who just couldn't take it any more.
The masks, the queues, the spacing,
the endless fears and speculating,
yet strangely Deliveroo at the door.

Another groundhog day of lockdown
people hearing but not being heard.
People not tasting but queerly seeing
and not touching those they've seen.
The medical staff and the bin men,
ideal heroes of a this new normal,
being clapped and cheered, congratulated,
and never given a bean.

Another groundhog day of lockdown,
the graph of dead forever rising,
care home lives frozen in aspic.
Scoping vaccines, hopes disarranging
diaries empty of any routine,
synapses, neurons over-operating
making ill those not yet sick.

Another groundhog day of lockdown,
false facts, fake news, new science,
and searching for clues from plagues past.
From biblical Egypt to the Romans,
to Black Death, Spanish Flu, nothing new
except guarantees this won't be the last.

A world of lepers the new normal,
separation, isolation, track and trace;
get the systems in place, make it formal,
keep it in mind for the next one we face.

Another groundhog day in lockdown…

SCHOOL MATES

by Brian Bourner

I was thinking about old school mates
But I couldn't remember their names
And I worried, what were their fates?
I was thinking about old school mates
And how forgetting their names was a shame
How decades on their faces remain the same.
I was thinking about old school mates
But I couldn't remember their names.

SELF CONTROL

by Sheila McDougall

She slapped her own hand

It was too much to bear

A mound of chocolate

Just sitting there tempting her

She'd come so far

And yet she had a mountain to climb

Or was it a slippery slope

The sponsor money was still rolling in

Exceeding all her expectations

Everyone believed in her

She walked away head held high

THE GRATE IS COLD

by Lucy Bucknall

The grate is cold. The Grate is Cold
The Yule log burnt to ash.
Untouched the milk and biscuits by the hearth.

For Father Christmas is no more,
And glad tidings of great joy
Have been destroyed
In this
The bleakest winter of them all.

The angel on the tree can only weep
To see how man has gone about his folly.

The mistletoe is fused and charred,
The holly, just a scar upon the wall.

Where once there was a wreath of green and red
There hangs a splintered crown; a symbol of the dead.

But hark, a herald's song floats from afar.
Outside I see the twinkle of a star
As night makes her retreat.

Am I awake or do I sleep?

My eyes, wide open now, delight to find
That Christmas is indeed divine.

For all that sadness and apocalyptic woe was but a dream
Wrought from my sleeping mind.

So down the crooked stairs I go,
On tips of toes, with bright anticipation.

Greeted by
The scent of pine,
The baubles on the tree,

The sweet elation
Caused by sounds of carols floating
From the kitchen radio
To wish us Yule-tide cheer.

What festive fare!
What joy!
What happy state of mind!

And then, our ears are locked on change in tone
And fear creeps on our skin.

We interrupt this broadcast to announce
That Russian bombs
With nuclear intent
Are heading for Great Britain and the West.

Take cover. Close your doors. Stay in.
God bless.

And thus we know,
Without the shadow of a doubt.
There is no saviour for mankind.

DIAMONDS LOST AND FOUND

by Helen Parker

At dawn the sea dons jewels that sparkle bright
and twinkle with reflection from the sun,
Each swell a diamond shifting with the light,
Each crest a necklace, gems with silver spun.

But should the smiling sun once hide her face
the diamonds, jewels and silver are all lost.
Of sparkling elegance there's now no trace,
like winter's drizzling grey dispelling frost.

By evening woodland creatures go to ground
but sunlight gives the sea a final wink.
The diamonds that were lost may now be found
as sunset paints the jewels a rosy pink.

The beauty of the jewel-clad ocean waves
can lift the hearts of emperors or slaves.

THE FOG

by Sylvia Simpson

Driving through the fog of uncertainty
Questions popped in my head like popcorn
Fear creeped up like a creepy crawly up my spine
Is this the end? What do I do?
Who do I call for support? Do I crawl into fear or do I stand bold
And face the challenges uncertainty brings?

Driving through the fog of loss
Every inch of me breaks
How I long to hold you once again
To hear your voice engaging me
Why? Why did death choose you?
The race cut short!
Do I crawl into depression?
Or do I finish the race we started?

Fog of poverty,
Fog of injustice
Fog of disability
Fog of the past, present and future
I will gather my strength and drive through you with endurance.

NO ROOM

by Sheila McDougall

Mary looked despondent
Joe had come back empty handed again
How difficult was it
There must be ice cream vans in December
She could taste the raspberry sauce
Dripping down the side
Suddenly she came to
The nurse was beckoning
The labour suite was ready

WINTER IS COMING

by Sheila McDougall

I'm praying for warm temperatures

Not record breaking perhaps

But mild enough

For central heating to stay dormant

And energy companies seething

As their profits drop

LADY LUCK or NOT EVERY DISABILITY IS VISIBLE

by Helen Parker

'You're so lucky, Tamsin.'
    'Yeah.' *Really?*
    'No covid, no bereavements, no family health scares. You didn't even have a reaction to your vaccines, right?'
    'Yeah.' *Not every disability is visible.*
    'Gemma's on the mend, finally, but still complains of brain fog. What's new?' He snickers. 'But since restrictions were lifted, there's no stopping her. She's at the gym twice a week, down the pub on Fridays, park run on Saturdays… But lockdown was awful.'
    'Yeah.' *It left an irreversible, gut-searing, throat-closing, lonely panic.*
    He looks at Tamsin's tiny front lawn. 'You're so lucky to have a garden.'
    'Yeah.' *Please leave.*
    'You should've seen Gemma! She was like a caged lioness, pacing round the flat, zooming her friends every evening, discussing the latest national and international statistics. She was quite hard to live with, though of course, don't tell her I said so. And now we're all free again, it's farewell to those mental health problems.'
    'Yeah.' *Who says it's OK not to be OK?*
    'They say there are school kids with mental health problems 'cos they've missed school. Ha! They should've enjoyed an extra holiday. I know I would've. Wouldn't you?'
    'Yeah.' *No.*
    'Now we're all off the leash, everyone'll be dashing off to the sun.' He looks at the book she has lent him. '*The Costa del Sol.* Thanks for this. So you'll be off somewhere next month? Got plans?'
    'Yeah.'

'Something special, eh?'
'Yeah.' *Either tablets or cord.*
'Lucky you!'

THE RIDER

by Brian Bourner

It was 10am at the empty end of January. For ten minutes Winston stood shivering next to the automatic check-out till. He glanced at his watch one last time before beginning to carefully unload the bottles from his wire basket, passing them over the glass barcode reader and placing them on the weighing platform. After each bottle "Approval Required" flashed on the screen against the item purchased. Winston soon felt the breath of the check-out till supervisor over his shoulder. He turned and looked into the face of an attractive young woman, glistening brown eyes, and wavy hair with pillarbox red streaks tied back in a ponytail. She was peering past him with a disapproving scowl, then briefly registering his haggard face, unshaven chin and sunken blue eyes. Winston's eyes drifted to the Tesco name badge above her chest - Kirstie McAllister.

"Yes, I am over eighteen," he felt obliged to say.

Kirstie flashed a card at the machine, pressed some buttons, and her face suddenly transformed into an early morning corporate smile. "Having a party?" she asked in a perfect 'Have a nice day' customer relations voice. She guessed Winston was late twenties, and saw him as quite cute in a bohemian kind of way with his stubble and his uncombed hair.

"Not me, the band," Winston explained.

"The band?"

"The Sleeping Tiger." Kirstie's blue eyes lit up on hearing the name. "Playing the O2 here tonight. First time in Scotland. Newcastle yesterday, Leicester the day before, Glasgow tomorrow. I'm Winston by the way. Been out trying to get this stuff since five o'clock this morning. Not unusual for the band to run out. Can normally find a 24 hour supermarket for a refill. Been tramping Edinburgh's freezing streets for ages. Petrol station guy finally told me there's no 24-hour booze seller in Scotland; you can't buy booze before 10am."

"Oh yes, that's right," Kirstie agreed. "And with Scotland's minimum unit alcohol pricing it's maybe that wee bit dearer too."

"If that's meant to deter over-indulgence it won't work for the boys in the band."

Kirstie glanced at the five bottles of tequila and said "No, I suppose not. That lot looks like it should keep them happy for a while though. Are you in the band?"

"I'm on the road with them, eh, Kirstie," he said, staring hard at her chest. "This will keep them going for a day at most. I'm the guy always gets sent to replenish the tour bus stocks. For some reason they call me the butler. But, hey, you're a roadie, you do what needs doing, don't you?"

"Expensive though."

"Not me though. The manager, Fat Jack, handles the money. He was a bit reluctant to hand some over this time. Don't know why. Reclaimed as part of the band's booking contracts. Part of their rider, specified in the small print. They forget. Jack makes sure. For the band's comfort, you know, keep them happy. You don't have any pewter mugs in the store?"

"Pewter mugs? Not something Tesco normally stocks. Or anywhere else in this shopping centre."

"Suppose Tesco might have done back in the old days of Thomas E. Stockwell and Jack Cohen, TES and CO you know."

"Oh, I see. No, I didn't."

"1962 before supermarkets were allowed to sell alcohol. When you do the band's shopping as a daily job you start thinking about shops, how all these supermarkets got started. The thing is, the band only drink tequila out of pewter mugs. Things got a bit lively on the tour bus last night. Mugs getting thrown about. Fat Jack got so worked up he chucked the mugs out the window as we crossed the Tweed. Pissed everyone off. Band might refuse to play tonight unless they get pewter mugs. Another job for the butler, eh? Checked my phone. Only one or two places do them in Edinburgh. I don't know the town – Jane Street? And I haven't got any transport."

"You've got a bit of a problem then," Kirstie said smiling. "Look, I've been on since six this morning. Part-time. Finish in half an hour. My old banger's outside. Maybe I can help you out? And, eh, any free tickets going spare for tonight's gig?"

A meaningful grin fought its way across Winston's grey face. "Sure, ok, a couple of tickets can be arranged. They'll be sleeping now; won't wake up till this afternoon's sound check. No point taking the tequila back to the bus without the mugs. I'll wait for you in Starbucks."

Kirstie appeared in the coffee-shop promptly, looking even more attractive without the Tesco shirt and badge. And she had obviously found time to apply a little make-up too. She ordered a small cappuccino at the counter and found him tucked into a corner behind a pillar. Winston was peering around nervously, tapping his fingers on the table. Seeing his agitation she drank the coffee quickly, said. "I can see you're in a hurry. Let's hit the road."

Kirstie's vintage Fiesta was scraped, dented, and looked ready for the scrapyard.

"Your car, you drive," said Winston, joking "I'll ride shotgun" as he got into the passenger seat beside her.

Despite its age the car still started first key turn and Kirstie pulled out of the shopping centre car park and headed for Leith full of excitement.

As Winston glanced out of the window moodily, seemingly wary of this unknown town, she switched on the radio and tuned in, as ever, to her favourite local music station, Radio Forth. The eleven o'clock news was just finishing when the mention of Sleeping Tiger caught her attention. Winston straightened up in his seat, his eyes watching her closely. Kirstie's eyes shot open as the newsreader reported that the band's manager had been found dead in a lane near the O2, the venue the band were due to play. Band members had been woken up on their tour bus and questioned by the police.

Kirstie turned to Winston, mouth agape, and the car swerved, almost colliding with a passing tram.

"Keep your eyes on the road!" Winston barked. "Shame about Jack", he added without emotion, "but he wasn't a nice man. The Tiger will find a better manager soon enough."

Kirstie pulled up in Jane Street and led Winston to the little shop, its window full of silver trophies yet to be won by anyone. Over-abundance of customers was clearly not a problem. On a wooden shelf sandwiched between two blank silver shields a small television was murmuring quietly to itself. A small elderly shopkeeper in a brown apron appeared behind the counter. With his gold skin and silver hair he looked more valuable than his stock. The television programme was interrupted for a news flash. The press had obviously followed quickly on the heels of the police.

A reporter in a heavy overcoat, its collar turned up, was saying that all those on the tour bus had disclaimed any involvement in their manager's, Jack Sukudry's, sudden death. They could all alibi each other. The police were clear that only the manager and one of the band's assistants had left the bus on its arrival at the venue. It had been Mr Sukudry's first time in the city and he was keen to form an idea of a venue's locale. Everyone else was left locked inside sleeping.

A tall gangly half-dressed man stood at the doorway of the tour bus with its blacked-out windows. The reporter introduced Sparky as as Mr Sparklington Holbein-Brown, the band's lead singer. Between yawns in sleepy voice Sparky said "I told the police it musta been some local hoodlum done it. Got his wallet didn't they. Apart from Jacko no-one went outside – well, there was that roadie I suppose." Sparky could not suppress a bout of throaty laughter. "Total alcoholic that roadie. Out scouting for booze. Drinks pints of tequila from a pewter mug. Total dipsomaniac. Hurled abuse at the manager last night after Jacko bawled at him to stop drinking or he was fired." There was a pause as it seemed to register with Sparky that he might have said something significant. He laughed nervously. "Here, where is that roadie? Jacko wasn't smashed over the head with a bottle of tequila was he?"

The reporter turned to a nearby policeman who at that point raised his eyebrows and glanced towards the taped off crime scene, an alley of slushy snow only a few yards from the tour bus, where shards of glass were embedded in a big pool of frozen dried blood. The reporter felt obliged to remind viewers that Edinburgh's O2 Academy had once been an abattoir.

Another bleary eyed man smoking a surprisingly long cigarette tumbled from the door of the bus and grabbed the microphone from the reporter's hand. "Here, what's going on now," he demanded, "bloody publicity session for a roadie?" The reporter managed to stay calm, and could be heard saying "Ah, very sorry to have disturbed you Mr Munchesterton, er, Munchy, er, on bass guitar, but…"

"That roadie – what a dinosaur," continued Munchy. "Told me it was natural he beat up his old lady for not bringing his booze fast enough so she ended up in hospital. Said she ran off after that. Hasn't been seen since. Said it was being left on his own made him want to join our crew. Said the police are still trying to find his girlfriend. Can't say I like him. I said to Sparky one time 'that roadie gets my goat'. And Jacko was passing and overheard. He got real angry – 'What right have you got to ask a tour assistant to get your coat?' – and after me and Sparky had stopped laughing he was always 'the butler'.

The microphone was wrestled from Munchy by another man wearing only shorts emerging from the bus. The reporter could only just be heard saying, "Ah, Mr Bertram FitzBisquet, er, Biscuits, the drummer if I'm not mistaken. Can you tell us anything of this 'butler'?"

"Nothin much,' Biscuits answered with a croaky voice. "A real drunk of a butler," he giggled. "You know, bit like Freddie Frinton in that classic old movie 'Dinner for One' - but not funny with it. Even sober, which isn't very often, he only talks bollocks about what shops sell what kinds of booze, when they started selling booze, the bloody retail history of booze."

At the shop counter Kirstie stood gaping at Winston, trembling. She started quickly towards the shop door. But Winston caught her arm, gripped it tightly, and dragged her back. He squinted at the shopkeeper and, between taut lips, said "Gimme a fuckin pewter mug!"

"And what kind of design were you…"

But Winston cut him off. "Any fuckin one. Just gimme it fast."

The shopkeeper gently placed a mug on the counter. Winston grabbed it with his free hand, making no attempt to pay and roughly hauled Kirstie out of the shop. With her shaking free hand Kirstie desperately rummaged in her pocket for her mobile phone. But Winston saw. He slapped the phone from her hand and stamped it into the pavement's slushy snow as he dragged her back to the car.

Forced behind the wheel Kirstie sat shaking, her ghost-like face a frightening contrast to bright red streaks of wavy hair. Winston left the passenger side door open. Keeping his eyes fixed on Kirstie he unscrewed the top of a bottle of tequila, poured a pint of it into the pewter mug, took a deep slug, and then crashed the almost empty bottle down on the kerb, leaving him holding the broken bottle by its neck as he slammed the door shut and pointed the jagged edges of the broken bottle at Kirstie.

The shop-keeper appeared in his doorway waving his hands as Winston yelled. "Get this shit-heap moving bitch. Time to have some fun."

A LOVELY SANDWICH

by Maitiu Corbett

Fred was a baker because he liked sandwiches. No, he lived sandwiches. Every day was just a grind punctuated by these humble, edible oases. If he hadn't been able to make them, he'd have probably starved.

The bread was the thing. Open crumb, tangy sourness, chewy crust. Of course, the more open the crumb, the more likely things were to escape. That was fine. He enjoyed chasing fillings around the plate or rescuing them from his lap. He gloried in the chaos of it. A sandwich with good integrity was a missed opportunity.

He grabbed the end of yesterday's loaf. The outer edge was a bit dried out, so he sliced it off and put it in the toaster. He reached again for his knife - because who can resist a slice of buttered bread before their toast? - and paused. Looking down at the newly exposed face, something was odd. He turned it upwards.

The burnished brown of the crust had laced itself through the loaf in all directions, making a toughened web. THANK YOU FOR THE LOVELY SANDWICH, said the message.

A day before it had been fantastically hot. And if you work in a bakery, you really understand what a heatwave is. The wide, stacked ovens belted out heat as Fred opened them in turn to slide loaves in and out. A blow to the chest from the middle one. A gut punch from the bottom. A haymaker finisher to the face from the top.

Fuck this, I need to get outside.
Even the hot day outside felt like a cold flannel across his forehead. He stood dazed for a minute, shielding his eyes

and enjoying the breeze. Across the street, the crypts and outcrops promised shade and otherworldly chill.

Sandwich first. *Something quick today.* Yesterday-Fred was a gent. Today-Fred took out the tupperware of flaked mackerel that Yesterday-Fred had mixed with chopped roasted red peppers, capers, lemon juice and black pepper the day before. A smear of Boursin, the fish mix, and a handful of rocket in a mini baguette and he had himself a fucking sandwich. Oh, and butter. Always butter.

"Who the hell opens a bakery across from a necropolis?" his sister had said. True, business wasn't exactly hectic, but he'd had his fill of hectic at the Crusty Loaf in town. Anyway, as far as he could tell, people seemed to come out of the necropolis hungry.

He hadn't even meant to sell sandwiches. A customer had once seen him tucking into one of his masterpieces - a humble jambon beurre as is happened - and just had to have one. Since then, Leven On The Edge had become known as "the bakery up by the necropolis that does the good rolls".

With today's monument to munch in hand, he strode up through the graves, feeling the dead cool spilling off them. He had his eye on a grand old crypt halfway up that had a big overhang and a great view across the valley.

'What's today's roll, boyo?' said Nancy as she held back her terrier.

'Sacred offering I'm afraid,' he said, tilting his head solemnly. 'Only the sandwich Gods dare gaze upon this one. And me, obviously'.

Nancy nodded sagely, arching her eyebrows so high they lifted the brow of her hat.

At last the mossy stone and jutting roof came into view. The crypt was dug into the side of the hill. Whoever had built it had clearly predicted this would be an elite sandwich spot, and had included a generous bench on the front wall. He sat and looked out at the rolling hills, scattered houses and, best of all, the little ant people basking in the sun like idiots. *Let them all burn to a crisp.*

He took out the chubby baton with a chef's flourish, holding it in both hands like a flute. He was about to bite when, from behind him, a growl. No, not a growl, more of a rumble. Not stone on stone, not wood on wood. It was unmistakable. A stomach grumble.

Fred froze, mouth gaping like a hungry chick, elbows shaking as he tried to maintain his purchase on the precious sandwich. He waited. *There's no way I heard a stomach grumble.* Then he heard it again, louder but also more echoed. Many more echoes than the crypt could possibly create.

Then the unmistakable smack of lips, echoed again like a stone cast into a cavern. *The sandwich*, he thought. *Leave the sandwich and go.*

Gently, he lowered the baguette to the seat beside him. Standing up slowly, he shuffled backwards down the steps.

A huge grumble, the biggest yet, sent a shockwave through the iron doors. Fred tripped backwards, recovered, and ran.

Looking at the crust-filigreed loaf, he shuddered. A couple of deep breaths. *It's a prank.* But he didn't really believe that. Still, he got himself under control.

The toast popped up. 'Fuck!' he bellowed.

Once his heart had stopped trying to strangle him, he stared back at the message. He stared for a long time.

Well, a customer is a customer.

So, at lunchtime he put together a couple of rolls - grilled halloumi, apricot jam, honey and pickled pink onions - and set off up the hill. He settled on the bench, tried to act natural, and waited.

It didn't take long. A low, earthy growl shook the stone beneath him. He tried his best to hold his nerve, set the sandwich down, and eat his. After two or three bites he judged that he had hit his bravery level for the day and got up to head back. Half way down the hill Nancy's dog jumped out and scared the skin off him.

The next day another message appeared.

EXCELLENT AGAIN. HAVE YOU CONSIDERED ADDING THYME TO THE JAM AND USING HOT HONEY?

Giving me notes now, eh? But, actually, that would probably be great. He'd give them a crack tomorrow.

And so it went for a couple of weeks. After a while, the new recipes came into rotation for the customers. There was no doubting that they worked - the looks of ecstasy on people's faces made him feel he was interrupting private moments.

On the third week, he could barely make it up the hill to the bakery after his early morning post-ovens break. People everywhere. *What are these idiots doing here? An accident? A massive funeral?* Maybe some celebrity had been caught pants-down up the hill.

As he got to the top, he saw that the queue started at his bakery.

'Um, what are you all doing here?'

'This place does awesome sandwiches man. They've got this one with egg mayo and truffled crisps, it's supposed to be fucking incredible.'

It was true. The truffle was the crypt ghost's idea. He got the keys out and started fumbling with the lock. Gasps erupted behind him and whispers of "that's him" and "he's smaller than I imagined".

He hadn't even made it behind the counter when they started flooding in. They rushed forward and the queue disintegrated. People started ordering things he'd made last week, or yesterday, or three days ago. In the din he heard strange combinations as orders crossed over each other:

"mortadella with... strawberry conserve"; "the one with crab... and Nutella".

For a few moments all he could do was stand there stunned. People started arguing. He had to get control of things.

'I haven't actually made anything yet!' he shouted, 'I haven't actually...'

They were too excited to hear him. Some people seemed to think he was taking orders from others further along, and elbowed their way towards him.

Fred clambered up onto the counter and said, as loudly and sternly as he could, 'everyone, please listen!'

Silence lurched into the room.

'I've just done my morning baking and I haven't actually got any sandwiches ready. You'll all have to come back after eleven.'

'That's alright mate, we'll wait.'

As he scurried around trying to make even half the sandwiches he'd need to feed his unruly congregation, they laid siege to him just beyond the threshold. When he had finally emptied his stock into the groaning sandwich cabinet, he let them in. He sold out in forty minutes, and had to send away at least twenty people.

The next day brought the same ravenous flock, and the day after. He had to call all his suppliers for emergency orders. All his ovens were used for sandwich bread, all his flour.

After service on the fourth day, one of the customers came back in.

'That really was a lovely sandwich.'

'Thank you very much,' said Fred, wiping his brow on his apron.

'I work for The Filter, do you know it?' she said.

He shrugged. 'No sorry.'

'No worries. We're an online paper. Got offices in like thirty-odd cities I think. I'd really like to interview you, if you wouldn't mind.'

He untied his apron. 'OK, I could do with a walk.'

They found a bench in the necropolis and she took out a phone and set it recording between them, giving him an awkward look.

'Oh, that's fine,' he said and she relaxed.

She took out a top-bound pad and a clicky pen. 'So, what's your name?'

They went back and forth on a few fundamentals. Where he was from; when he opened the bakery; why he had opened next to a load of graves.

'Because I could afford it. Do you know what it's like trying to get a shop in town?'

Then the main question.

'Where do you get the ideas for your sandwiches?'

'A ghost tells me them,' he said.

She laughed at that. 'Seriously though, peanut butter and pickles?'

His experiment with the truth couldn't last. 'Yeah, that's a weird one a friend from college liked' he lied.

She leaned in, looking about conspiratorially. 'Strange that you should mention ghosts. Did you know who is buried here?'

He shrugged.

'Donato Di Matteo,' she said, with a triumphant look.

He looked blankly back at her.

'Oh sorry, I assumed he was a person that sandwich makers know. He was this crazy sandwich guy in Sicily like 50 years ago. In Syracuse I think. He was a bit of a maverick apparently.'

'How did he end up here?'

'Love, of course.'

He put a note in with the next sandwich: "Nice to meet you Donato. I'm Fred."

The next day his bread read: A PLEASURE ALSO TO MEET YOU FRED. BUT, AH, IT IS SINGOR DI MATTEO, PLEASE.

IT WISNAE ME
(Tales from a Working Life no.7)

by John Tucker

Mike was the foreman in charge of these building refurbishments. The hospital isolation block was completed and the squad was getting ready to do the next block that had been emptied by the hospital staff. The keys had already been given to Mike.

Mike said "Billy, get the other two apprentices to help you." Pointing to a big heap of gear needed for the job he said, "This is the equipment you'll need. Take it to the next standalone block right at the top of the hill. Follow the one-way single track road that runs between the two sections of grass parkland on either side of the road."

Billy found a hospital trolley. It had four pneumatic mini-wheels that supported a wooden platform six feet long by four feet wide. The front two wheels were controlled by the pulling loop handle bar. Billy and one of the apprentices pulled while the other apprentice pushed from the rear.

It was heavy going getting up the hill. When fully loaded with equipment and tools the load caused a lot of bad language, sweat and groaning, but they reached the top of the hill and got it all unloaded.

Some time later, when all the work was done and all three were very tired, Billy looked at the empty trolley and said "If I sit at the front and use both hands to lean the pulling bar forward I can steer the trolley and we can all ride back on it to the starting point. It's all downhill. Jump on! Lets go!"

Ah, but it's a problem when cruising down a one-way road in the wrong direction, especially with no brakes. Even worse is when a bus with an angry driver is approaching from the other direction and he's over-working his horn. Billy had no alternative but to veer off the road and mount the newly cut grass of the parkland.

But the grass-cutting tractor driver, who had been neatly making haystacks alongside the road for ease of uplifting, watched them being demolished by the joyriders and was not amused. He added his horn to the cacophony of noise invading the quiet hospital grounds as the apprentices sped on, only to eventually grind to a halt in front of Mike the foreman.

What was that all about?" demanded Mike.

"*It was him*" said the apprentices in unison, pointing at Billy.

'Well, I suppose that makes a change', thought Billy. 'It's usually just *It wisnae me.*' But he was not looking forward to Mike catching up with him later for his well-deserved cuff round the ear and sanctimonious lecture on health and safety.

IN DAYS OF COVID

by Brian Bourner

Jiggered by jigsaws and knackered by Netfix,
climbing the walls and scared by statistics,
hair like a hooligan, video calling in bed,
finding a mask just to buy beer and bread.
Sending for fat, sugar, and a cyclist to deliver,
paying only with plastic now no-one wants silver.
Schools shut, shops shut and students shut up,
actors, musicians, and publicans bottom-up,
while Westminster MPs still flap their oars,
behind the tide's curve where wild waters roar,
leaving white coats to offer a horizon of hope
for culture, sport, life, still onward they grope
under hospitalised black skies vultures descend
on family, neighbours, loved ones and friends.
Groundhog days stress-test old Parkinson's Law
or suffer long shadow pain, gripped in its maw.

Blue tits and butterflies, pollution-free roads,
neighbourhood wandering, and finding new modes
for home-made cooking, and make meals sparky,
for reading weird books, hearing music that's quirky,
seeing clouds in the sky and stars in the night,
holiday hassles forgotten, no packing no flights.
For now is always the time, the time of your life,
it can be what you make it with love or with strife.

TREASURE

by Helen Parker

The Sunday evening bus was full of travellers grey and weary
The weekend's end and threat of work had left them sad and dreary.
While darkness fell and silence reigned most people read their phones,
Some work-bound, night-shift folk, but most were heading to their homes,
When in came, in a flurry, Mrs Jones, all pink and anxious,
Awakening the passengers, enlivening their blankness.

'My goodness me!' said she, 'I really don't know what to do!
I left my shopping on the bus. My phone was in there, too.
I cannae phone the company – I'll have to go tomorrow.'
Upset and flustered, Mrs Jones had lost all her bravado.

The driver scratched his balding head. 'The bag,' he said, 'What colour?'
'A sort of yellow,' she explained, 'with Sainsbury's on the cover.'
'Okay, so when was this?' he asked, 'Which bus route? This is 7.'
But Mrs Jones was all wound up. 'My oranges and lemons,
My milk and cheese, my bread and peas,' she wailed, 'they'll all be rotten!'

'Never you mind,' the driver soothed, 'such things are oft forgotten.
But look behind you on the rack – is that what you'll be wanting?'
And there, abandoned on the bus, the Sainsbury's bag lay yawning.

She looked inside and jumped for joy, despite advancing age.
'Why yes!' she crowed and lifted it from out its metal cage.
'God bless you, driver dear,' she sang, 'you've saved my eggs and bacon.
That bag has got a week's supply of yogurt, cream and cake in.'

By now the bus was full of smiles, of people sharing pleasure,
They shared surprise, delight and joy, like finding buried treasure.

This story isn't mine to tell – it's Ingrid's – she's our tenant.
She skipped home happily that night, her mood became quite buoyant.
Our mother tongue's not hers, you see, she speaks which she prefers –
Norwegian, French and English too, an able raconteuse.

WEEKEND AWAY

by Janice Gardner

'That's us all packed and ready to hit the road,' Lynn said to her cousin Annie.

'I'm looking forward to this. I'm still not sure if camping is for me,' Annie sighed.

'It's not camping its glamping. Posh camping to be precise,' Lynn added with a smile.

'I certainly liked what you showed me on the website. Let's get going,' said Annie rubbing her hands together.

'It's about time you put your ex behind you and enjoy life.'

'Thanks for putting up with me and persevering.'

'I'm so glad you agreed in the end to come on this trip. Poor Jim unexpectedly got a bad bug.'

They climbed into Lynn's white Jeep and headed north. They were soon leaving Edinburgh and driving over the Queensferry Crossing, driving up the A9 heading north.

'The mountains are spectacular. Wow they are so amazing. Look at the sun sparkling over them,' Annie looked out the window as they drove on.

'I've been up and down this road so many times I take the mountains for granted.' Lynn's eyes were focused ahead.

'That doesn't look good,' Lynn leaned forward and peered through the front windscreen.

'Oh dear, that looks like an unexpected storm on the horizon. I think we should check out the weather forecast,' Annie leaned forward and switched on the radio.

'Wow it's almost a white out. We can't go on in this,' said Lynn slowing down.

'Look there's a farm,' Annie lifted her hand and pointed.

'Let's pull in and see if there's anyone at home.' Lynn slowed the Jeep and drove cautiously up the long narrow track. 'That snow is getting heavy now. I'm not too happy about this.'

'It's not what I was expecting. Thank goodness there's a light on, at least someone's home.'

'I didn't see this in the weather forecast.'

'Neither did I. I'll go over to the front door and see who is at home. I won't be long.' Annie jumped out and hurried over to the farmhouse.

She knocked at the door and waited. Music could be heard indoors, then the sound of footsteps coming towards the door. A tall handsome red-headed man opened the door.

'Hi, I'm sorry to trouble you. We're heading up to Inverness and have been caught in this unexpected weather. Is it possible we could spend the night here?' asked Annie.'

'I'm Archie,' he held out his hand introducing himself.

'Pleased to meet you,' Annie smiled up at him taking his hand.

'I realise the weather is bad and I have a huge house,' he said, running his long fingers through his curly hair. 'However, my wife has left me, and I have neighbours who would talk if I let females stay in the house.'

'No problem. We don't want to come in. We'll be more than happy to shelter under any cover. Are there any outbuildings? Hopefully the weather will improve overnight, and we'll be gone by first light.'

'There's an open barn over to the left.' He stepped forward and pointed. 'Do you need me to come over and help?'

'No, it's okay thanks. You don't want to come out in this horrible weather. Thanks again,' she called over her shoulder as she walked back to Lynn.

'How did you get on?' asked Lynn running down her window.

'Great. The farmer, Archie, said we could shelter in the barn.'

'Anywhere is better than out in this storm. Can you watch me while I reverse in.'

'Sure,' said Annie following the Jeep.

'At least there is plenty of room for us in the car. You can make yourself comfortable in the back if you like,' said Lynn.'

'Thanks, that suits me fine.'

They settled for the night and awoke to see the sun shining,

'I can't believe how quick the snowstorm has and passed over,' said Annie

'That what happens up this way in the Highlands. Now it's time to get organised,' said Lynn stretching her shoulders. 'At least we can have a shower at the glamping site. Do you think the Archie will let us use the loo before we go?'

'I'll nip over and ask. Give me a minute.'

Lynn waited and heard a tractor moving off. Annie signalled with a wave and walked towards Lynn.

'Archie has had to go out in the tractor. He's quite happy for us to go indoors. He's shown me around. Let's get our toilet bags and head over now.'

'That was very kind of him.'

'Yes,' smiled Annie.

They were soon ready and heading northwards to their destination.

'You wouldn't have believed the weather could change so much. This sunshine is so uplifting,' said Annie as they drove along the quiet road that threaded through the countryside.

'I must admit you're a lot brighter today. It's good to see you looking to happy.'

'I'm loving this unexpected break,' she smiled watching sheep and lambs grazing in the fields.

'Shame poor Jim got a last-minute bug and couldn't come. Glad you agreed to come instead.'

'Look, the sign for the glamping site.We should be there in five minutes or so,' said Lynn.

'Wow this is amazing,' said Annie as they drove slowly up the drive.

They were met by the host and taken to their glamping tent.

'What do you think?' Lynn asked standing back holding the door open.

'It's far bigger than I imagined. I love it,' said Annie stepping in looking around.

'Let's enjoy our holiday and get exploring.'

'Glamping is great fun. I will certainly want to come and do this again.'

'I'll happily come with you,' said Lynn.

'The scenery and the wildlife are amazing. I've taken so many brilliant photos.'

'We'll have a good night's sleep then get up early to avoid rush hour traffic.'

'Sounds like a plan.'

In no time they were driving back to Edinburgh enjoying the bright sunny day.

* * *

About a year later, Lynn received an unexpected letter from a legal office. It took a few minutes for her to realise that it was from a solicitor acting for Archie, the kind farmer that had let them shelter on his farm when they hit the snowstorm.

Later that day Lynn called round to see Annie. 'Do you remember Archie, the good-looking man from the farm who let us stay last year when we ran into the snowstorm?'

'Yes, I do,' smiled Annie.

'Did you happen to get up in the night, go over to the house and pay him a visit?'

'Well, yes,' she said, a little embarrassed about being found out. 'Your snoring woke me up and I went for a stroll. Archie was out with his dog.'

'So, you saw him?'

'Yes, in fact I must admit we kept in touch and met up quite a few times for about six months. Then he just disappeared. No word. Nothing.'

'Did you happen to give him my name instead of yours?'

Annie's face turned bright red as she spoke. 'Yeah look, I'm sorry, I did.'

'Why did you do that?'

'Oh, it was a silly quick decision. As his wife had left him, I wasn't too sure about him. After all the trouble I had with my ex. It was our first time and I never thought I'd see him again.'

'But you did.' Lynn raised her eyebrows.

'Yes. He was really a lovely guy. I was going to let him know what I'd done, but then we lost contact.'

'Well now we know why he lost touch.'

'What are you talking about?'

'Here.' Lynn handed her the letter. 'I received this letter from his lawyer.'

'He died,' Annie gasped, looking up at Lynn,

'Apparently so, after a short illness.'

'As the letter says. He wants to leave everything to the most special person he has ever known. Lynn Greer.'

'You,' Annie's hand went to her throat.

'You told him you were Lynn Greer,' she said laughing.

SPEAKING OF THE DEAD

by Brian Bourner

(1)
Jock said when it came to his turn
He would rather be buried than burn
But costs were obscene
So forgoing his dream
He now sits on the shelf in an urn

(2)
It's all there on social media she said
Bisexuals, transgenders, three in a bed.
Invading the privacy
Of every wee lassie
Those young lads still alive should be dead.

(3)
Alimony is late and I'm alone
With only a number I was shown.
It's a pity of course
Couldn't really be worse
Because you can't get blood out a phone.

(4)
She said she could not keep to deadlines
And keep her hair dyed like fire engines
But painting a wall
Her ladders did fall
In red paint and her dead head made headlines

NOTES ON AUTHORS

Brian Bourner is Edinburgh born and bred and has spent most of his life there apart from some years in London and Sheffield. He has worked as a chartered banker, chartered librarian, and social researcher. He has written a novel, several books of short stories, several volumes of poetry, and three short nonfiction books about aspects of Edinburgh.

Lucy Bucknall was brought up in Scotland before moving to central France where she worked as an English Language teacher for almost thirty years. She has recently taken up a new role as houseparent in the private boarding school sector and enjoys spending her free time exploring the Moray coast, where she now lives and works.

Maitiu Corbett is originally from Edinburgh and now lives and works in Glasgow. He loves reading and writing anything strange, be it fantasy, sci-fi or odd cousins of either. A previous publication was a short story put out as a Medium publication (See: https://medium.com/ pure-fiction/thorns-d7a4b1fd2313)

Ian Elliott is from East Lothian and enjoyed a career working in electrics and electronics. Since retiring his family have encouraged him to start writing down the story of his life.

Annie Foy began writing in mid-life. She writes short pieces for performance at spoken word events, mostly but not exclusively in Edinburgh, Glasgow and East Lothian. She also writes flash fiction and short stories for publication.

Janice Gardner loves writing and has done so for many years with articles and fillers for UK newspapers and magazines. She has also written for English speakers' newspapers and magazines in Greece and Cyprus. Recently, she has been having fun writing short stories that have been published here in the UK.

Jamie Hafner is from rural Pennsylvania in the United States and is currently studying for a postgraduate degree.

Robin King is an ancient scribe.

Sheila McDougall is a retired librarian having spent her working life in university, college and school libraries. Having a short attention span she prefers writing poetry and the odd flash fiction. She is still seeking her inner Pam Ayres.

Helen Parker has published several books for children, a first novel for adults in 2018, and several of her short stories have appeared in literary magazines including *Gutter* and *Mslexia*. She has travelled widely in the Middle East and holds a master's degree in creative writing.

Valentina Romanazzi is Italian and currently works in retail administration in Edinburgh.

Gracie Rose, from Largs, is a student in the final year of her astrophysics degree and loves writing in her free time. She usually writes short stories and occasionally poetry. She plans to start working on a novel when she has more time.

Sylvia Simpson is originally from Belize. She now lives with her family in Edinburgh and is studying midwifery.

Rebecca 'Bex' Stevenson is fond of both dogs and writing.

Georgina Tibai came to Edinburgh from Hungary a decade ago, initially working as a child carer and a croupier. She studied for entry qualifications at Edinburgh College and graduated from Edinburgh Napier University. She is now a British citizen and working in education.

John Tucker is Edinburgh born and bred and has always lived in the city. He worked for many years as an electrician and started writing only after retirement. He likes to write humorous stories.

Stéphanie Voytier is French and arrived in Scotland in 2010. She discovered the joy of writing when a health condition kept her housebound for more than a year. She attended an online course on writing children's fiction, and since then she has been working on a story set in the western Highlands and largely inspired by her love for nature.

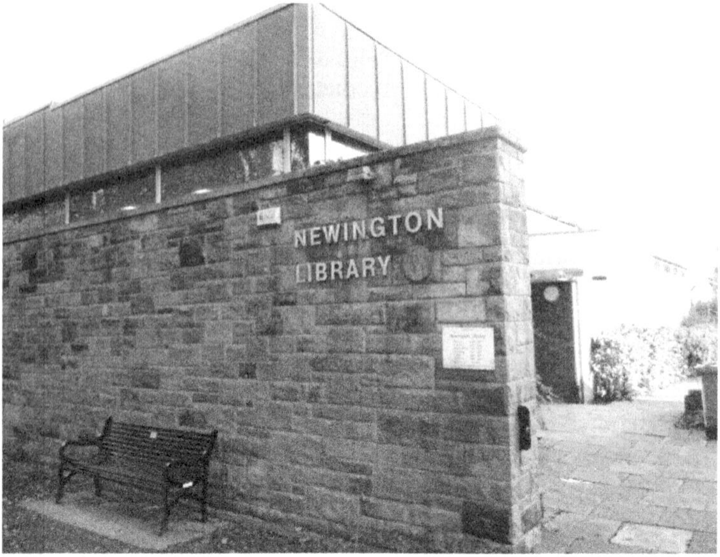
NEWINGTON
LIBRARY

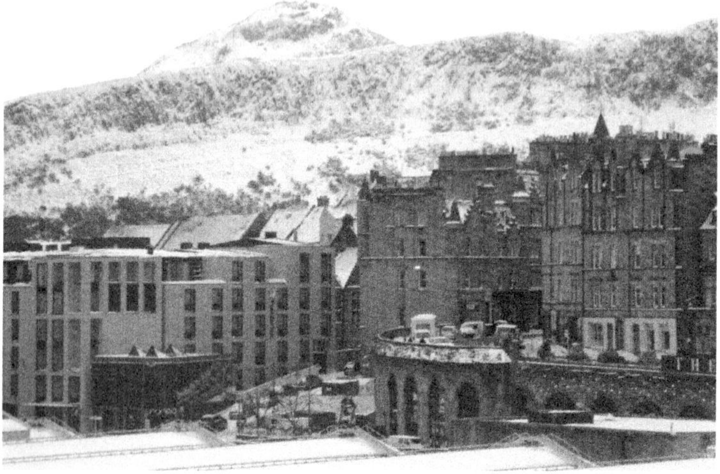

NOTES ON AUTHORS

Printed and bound by CPI Group (UK) Ltd, Croydon, CR0 4YY
13/11/2023
03575248-0001